Appalachian

Winter

Hauntings

Edited By
Michael Knost and Mark Justice

Woodland Press, LLC

III

Introduction

I grew up in a small coal camp in southern West Virginia, way back in the paveless hollow known as Dempsey Branch of the Appalachian Mountains. Holidays were special to me because we didn't have much money, but Mom and Dad always made sure I had a good Christmas. They both worked long hours, many times sacrificing their own wants or needs, to ensure I would love the presents Santa Claus left under the tree.

I caught on to the Santa story faster than most children my age. I saw too many holes in the stories and I asked too many hard questions. My Dad finally told me I was correct, there was no such thing as a jolly old elf named St. Nick. That's when Christmas really came *alive* for me.

I began distorting the Santa legend in conversations with my friends and schoolmates. I'd tell them there was a reason Santa left a lump of coal for naughty children: he'd intended to use the coal in a fire to burn them! I told them Santa's elves (the little critters that made the toys) were demons . . . and they have been known to eat unworthy children Santa delivered toys to on Christmas.

Well, as you can imagine, this made many of my schoolmates terribly frightened, as they may not have been on their best behavior at all times. In fact many of them went home and relayed to their parents what I'd told them, admitting they were now afraid of Santa and his rabid reindeer.

I was in so much trouble it was not even funny.

But it was worth it. I think that was when I realized I loved storytelling and making people cry, of course. Who would have ever dreamed I would grow up to be a horror writer?

Working with Mark Justice on this project has been a great experience, as I realize he was as sick and demented growing up as I was.

With this project, our goal was to find stories that were appropriate to the Appalachian region, and also relative to the heart of the Christmas spirit we grew up around. What we found were stories that followed the guidelines yet broke all other conventional molds. I think you'll like them.

Oh, and a word of caution: demonic elves love to sneak up on people as they read scary books.

Enjoy the stories!

Michael Knost
Logan County, WV

*   *   *

Since I was a child, hauntings and holidays have been inexorably linked.

Perhaps it's because when I was growing up, ghosts seemed to be a big part of the Christmas season. For weeks before the big day, I would encounter almost daily reference to Scrooge's trio of specters. I was always told I needed to be filled with the Christmas spirit.

(I also wasn't all that old when I made the shocking realization that Santa was just Satan with the letters scrambled. And they both wore red. You can bet little Mark had a few sleepless nights after that revelation. But I digress.)

So I learned early on that it was perfectly normal for shades, wraiths, and phantasms to hang around the mistletoe and stockings. Their company became as familiar as the toy section in the Sears catalogue.

When Michael Knost and I first talked about projects we would like to do together, *Appalachian Winter Hauntings* came to the top of the list. So the call went out and we were answered by some of the finest writers in the genre.

It's been a pleasure to work with some of my favorite authors, including Scott Nicholson, Beth Massie, Ronald Kelly, Steve Vernon, and Steven J. Tem. And an unexpected pleasure has been the joy upon discovering so many fine writers whose names will probably be new to you. I just wish we had room to showcase every amazing story we encountered.

Finally, you may be wondering about the Appalachian setting.

Okay, it's confession time. Despite my advanced age and encroaching decrepitude, and a lifetime of hard-earned cynicism, I still love Christmas. There has always been something magical about the season. To me, no place is as filled with that magic as a small, tight-knit mountainside community.

So pour a steaming mug of hot cocoa (or something stronger if you're easily frightened), wrap your favorite blanket around you, and imagine a small farmhouse, nestled in the shadows of rolling hills. A light snow is falling. The lights have gone out. The family is asleep. But inside those walls, there is movement. Something has come back. Something bearing gifts.

Be careful when you open this present ...

Mark Justice
Them Thar Hills

Table of Contents

X

1

The Peddler's Journey

By Ronald Kelly

"Tell us, Grandpa!"

Chester McCorkendale shared his little brother's enthusiasm. "Yeah, come on, Grandpa," he urged, sitting on the threadbare rug before the hearth. "Tell us the story about the Ghostly Peddler!"

Grandpa eyed the boys with ancient eyes and smiled. He took a puff on the brier pipe he clutched in yellowed dentures and let the blue smoke roll from his nostrils like dragon's breath. "Ah, you boys have heard that old tale every Christmas Eve since you were knee-high to a grasshopper."

"But we want to hear it again," David demanded. "It's like a ... you know, whaddaya call it?"

"Tradition," his big brother told him. "Come on, Grandpa. Nobody tells it like you do."

Grandpa McCorkendale chuckled and leaned back in his hickory wood rocker, causing it to creak dryly. He glanced around the cramped main room of the cabin. The crackling fire cast a warm, orange glow over the walls papered with newsprint, the stones of the hearth, and the long, dangling stockings that drooped from the mantle; stockings that had been darned by their Ma a half dozen times or so. Yes, this was the place to tell the old story again, and most certainly the time.

Grandpa couldn't help but string them along a bit further, though. "Are you sure you want ghost stories and not "The Night Before Christmas" or the birth of Jesus? I'll just go filling your head full of haints and horrors, and you boys'll never get to sleep tonight."

"Are you gonna tell it or what?" snapped David, rolling his eyes.

Chester elbowed his brother sharply. He didn't want David to cross the fine line between childish pestering and disrespecting an elder. That was one thing Grandpa, no matter how patient he was, would not tolerate. There was no need to go fishing for a hide-tanning… especially on Christmas Eve.

Grandpa's eyes sparkled. "All right. I won't leave you waiting any longer. Your Ma and Pa's done gone to bed, and you'd best get nestled beneath the quilts yourself." He grinned around the stem of his pipe. "Besides, if Ol' Saint Nick can't make it this year, 'cause of this dadblamed Depression and all, then the Ghostly Peddler might just show up, bearing gifts."

The very thought of the mountain ghost standing before their hearth sent a delicious chill shivering through their bones. They lay on their bellies on the horsehair rug, their chins planted in their palms, waiting for the storyteller to begin.

Grandpa puffed on his pipe a moment more, staring almost dreamily into the blue haze of tobacco smoke. "They say it happened in the winter of 1869. The cannons that echoed violently down in the valley during the War Betwixt the States had scarcely been silent four years when the old man showed up at the township of Maryville. He was an Irishman, burly and quick with a smile and a joke, his hair and whiskers the color of rusty door hinges. No one knew the feller's name, just knew that he toted a pack upon his back full of medicines and notions, and some wooden toys he'd whittled with a sharp blade and a steady hand. There was no general store in Maryville at the time, just a way station that doubled as a tavern and inn. The Peddler, as folks called him, showed up that late December, brimming with songs and stories and a belly big enough to hold his share of beer and bourbon when the menfolk of the village were generous enough to buy him a round or two."

Grandpa paused and eyed his two grandsons. "Now, I ain't boring you, am I? You're not feeling too sleepy to go on, are you?"

"No, sir!" the boys chimed in together.

The elderly man nodded and went on. "Well, it was nigh on to Christmas Eve, when the Peddler heard tell of a child up in these Tennessee mountains. The boy had fallen beneath a logging wagon and his leg had been shattered, broken in three places. The old peddler was a man of great heart and he felt compassion for the crippled boy. He also learned that the family was hard-hit with poverty. They were dirt-floor poor with scarcely two nickels to rub together."

"So what'd he do, Grandpa?" asked David, although he had heard the story many times before.

"Well, what he did was get out his whittling knife and a slab of white oak and he went to work. The crowd at the tavern grew silent as they watched him carve the most skillfully-crafted figure of a running stallion that they ever did seen. It was common knowledge that the lame boy on the mountain was a lover of horses, although he and his family had none to call their own. So the Peddler carved this here toy horse out of wood. Lordy Mercy, they said the little stallion looked so life-like that it might have galloped across the tabletop with oaken hooves, if the old man had possessed the magic to breathe such life into it.

"Well now, the folks there in the tavern tried to talk the Peddler out of it, but he got it in his head that he should take that toy to the crippled child that very night. It had snowed the majority of the day and it was awful cold outside. But no matter how much they argued with him, the Peddler's heart proved much bigger than his common sense. He bundled up, lifted his pack, and ventured out into the frigid darkness. Having gotten the directions to the boy's cabin from the barkeep, he began his long, dark journey into the foothills, and then onward

3

toward the lofty peaks of the Appalachians."

A German clock on the stone mantelpiece chimed the hour of nine. "Are you sure you young'uns ain't hankering to get to bed? You've had a busy day and you look plumb tuckered out."

"No, sir!" they said, their eyes wide with anticipation. "Please, go on."

Grandpa drew on his pipe again. "Very well... but here is where the spooky part comes along. You see, that peddler got as far as Gimble's Gap and was suddenly trapped in the worse snowstorm the mountains had seen in a month of Sundays. The blizzard was so cold and icy, and its wind so blustery, that the Peddler couldn't see three feet in front of him. But still he had it in his mind to visit the boy that very night and he trudged onward, through the driving flurries and deep drifts. Somewhere along the way, he lost his way. He could have turned back right then and there, and probably made it to the tavern alive. But the Peddler was a stubborn feller and he continued his night's journey through the icy darkness with that wooden horse clutched in one gloved hand. But the struggle of stepping through the high drifts and the force of the winter wind pushing against him took its toll. It wore him plumb out and slowed him down considerably."

"But he never got there, did he, Grandpa?" asked Chester, although he already knew the answer.

"No, Grandson, he never did. His journey up the mountain was in vain. Some of the men from the tavern grew concerned and the following morning, after the blizzard had subsided, they took off up the mountain, looking for him. On about the afternoon of Christmas Day, they found him, frozen to the trunk of a deadfall. They said he was a gruesome sight to behold! His clothing was icy and as hard as stone. His curly red beard was now snowy white, his rosy face was pale and blue, and even his eyeballs were covered over with frost. The old man was dead, having grown exhausted from his treacherous journey and frozen to death on the trunk of that fallen sycamore."

Grandpa's eyes narrowed a bit, a peculiar look crossing his wrinkled face. "However, there was one strange thing they noticed before they pried his carcass from the log and carried him back down the mountain. The hand that had clutched the wooden horse was empty now... and in the snow, leading away from the dead body of its creator, were the prints of tiny hooves."

Chester and David shuddered in wondrous fright. "So that was the end of the tale?"

"No, by George!" proclaimed Grandpa. "For, you see, every Christmas Eve, the Ghostly Peddler roams the hills and hollows of these here mountains, in search of that wooden horse. The spirit of that stubborn Irishman still has it in his mind to find that wandering pony and give it to its rightful owner... that crippled boy from long years past.

"But as he makes that lonesome journey, his benevolence still rings as clear as a church bell. He leaves toys, carved by his ghostly hand, in the stockings of the young'uns of these Tennessee mountains, if only for the chance to warm his frozen bones by their midnight fire."

The boys grinned at each another. "Do you think the Peddler will leave us something tonight?" asked David.

Grandpa tamped out the dregs of his pipe, laid it on the arm of his rocking chair, and stood up. His joints popped as he stretched. "I wouldn't doubt you boys finding a play-pretty in your stockings come daybreak. But he ain't gonna come with you up and about. Best dress for bed and snuggle beneath those covers. He oughta be roaming the mountains on around midnight, looking for that wooden stallion."

Both boys hopped up from the floor, eager to get to sleep. "Goodnight, Grandpa," they said, heading for their parents room and the little bed they shared there.

"Goodnight, boys," he said, heading for the third room of the cabin and his own bed. "And a very Merry Christmas to you both."

Before long, they had settled into the comfort of feather mattress, beneath toasty patchwork quilts, and drifted into their separate slumbers. The mountain cabin grew still and quiet. The only sounds to be heard were the crackling of the fire in the hearth and the lonesome howling of a winter wind outside the frosted windowpanes.

A little before midnight, Chester crept from his bed, careful not to rouse his sleeping brother. The story of the Ghostly Peddler was fresh and alive in his mind. Knowing that he really oughtn't to do it, he left the bedroom and snuck across the main room, past the hearth. He took up sentry behind his grandfather's high-backed rocker, tucked, unseen, in the shadows just behind.

Chester waited for what seemed to be a very long time. He did not feel the least bit sleepy, though. He crouched there, watching intently, his ears straining for the least little sound. Once or twice, he thought he heard something scamper across the roughly-hewn boards of the plank floor, but knew that it was probably the mouse that had taken up residence there in the cold months prior to Christmas; the rodent who had helped itself to their cornmeal and winter cheese, much to Ma's displeasure.

Finally, the clock chimed the hour of twelve. Chester sat there in breathless anticipation, listening, watching through the pickets of the old rocking chair. He heard a noise in the cabin... the mouse again, he first thought. But, no, it seemed to originate from something a mite larger than a mouse; more like a muskrat or a chipmunk, perhaps.

And the tiny footfalls were odd, too. They sounded more like small clopping, than the skittering of sharply-nailed animal feet upon the floorboards.

For several minutes, Chester sat there. He listened intently, but could hear nothing else. Then, abruptly and without warning, the cabin door burst open. A gust of icy wind, laden with snowflakes as big as goose feathers, blew inside, causing the flames of the hearth to gutter and snap. Then, with the winter's draft, appeared a broad form. He stepped into the cabin and, just as suddenly as before, the pine door closed shut.

Chester's heart thundered in his young chest. There, standing in the center of the main room, was a burly man dressed in icy rags. His broad face was pale blue in color and his hair and beard were covered with frost and jagged icicles. It was the man's eyes that terrified the boy, though. They looked about the room, the orbs frozen and coated with a thin sheen of ice, the pupils barely visible.

So the old stories were true. It was him at last… the Ghostly Peddler!

Chester watched, transfixed in horror, as the spirit crossed the room. He crouched a bit, as though searching the floor for something. That peculiar sound echoed again … the rat or whatever it was.

"I hear ye now," rasped the ghost in a coarse whisper. "Ye'd best not try to hide from me, little one. Your shoeprints have led me to this very door."

Chester wasn't at all sure whom the Ghostly Peddler was talking to, until the old man reached between the woodbox and his mother's sewing basket and brought something out into the firelight. He watched in utter amazement as the spirit held the tiny creature aloft. It was a small, wooden stallion, bucking and whinnying, as it struggled to escape the icy grasp of the Peddler's gloved hand.

"Gotcha!" laughed the old man in triumph. "After all these years, I'm at journey's end."

Chester watched as the ghost walked to the stone hearth. It was there that an incredible transformation took place. The old peddler stood before the glow of the crackling flames, seeming to drink in its golden warmth. The icy

7

exterior of the apparition slowly melted away, revealing a robust Irishman wearing a worn tweed suit coat, britches, walking boots, and a brown derby hat. His face grew rosy, his beard its true color of rusty redness, and his eyes sparkled a brilliant hazel green. A grin crossed his ruddy face and he sighed contentedly.

"Tis grand to be amongst the living again," he said aloud. "If only for a wee time."

Chester watched as the Peddler set the wooden stallion on the stone mantle. The tiny horse reared defiantly, flashing its small hooves and snorting in frustration. Then it trotted to and fro, down one end of the stone ledge to the other. The old man opened his leather pack and took several wooden toys from inside; a top, building blocks, a couple of soldiers brandishing muskets, and cavalry swords. He deposited them in the boys' stockings, nodding to himself in satisfaction.

When he spoke again, he spoke not to himself, but to Chester.

"I know you're there, lad," he said. "Peering at me from behind the chair. Come here, will ye? I wish to entrust a very special gift unto your care."

Curiously, Chester rose and walked toward the hearth. Strangely enough, the ghostly Irishman who stood before the fire did not frighten him. When he came within six feet of the old man, the Peddler took the horse from the mantle and extended it to him. "See to it that young Johnny receives this present, will ye not? I meant for him to have it a very long time ago ... but, alas, the journey here was much further than I could have ever imagined."

"Yes, sir," said Chester. He reached out for the stallion, but it whinnied and snapped at him with its tiny oaken teeth.

"Go on. Take it now. It'll not harm ye, boy."

Chester took hold of the squirming animal and, the moment his fingertips touched it, the stallion became no more than a wooden toy again.

"I'm much obliged to ye," said the Peddler with a courteous tip of his bowler.

Chester stepped back a few feet and watched as the ghost closed his eyes, breathed deeply, and beamed a great smile. "My work here is done," he said softly. "Dear Father, take me hither to me heavenly home." Then his burly form grew as bright and brilliant as a white-hot horseshoe in a blacksmith's forge. The Peddler seemed to dissolve into a thousand fiery cinders, which swirled about the cabin for a frantic moment, then flew up the dark channel of the stone chimney and skyward into the snowy night.

Chester stood there for a moment, dazed. He looked down at his flannel nightshirt and his bare feet and wondered if it had only been a dream … that perhaps he had merely been sleepwalking. But then he looked at the stockings filled with toys and the wooden stallion in his hand and knew for a fact that it had all taken place.

He heard movement behind him and turned to find Grandpa standing there in the doorway of his bedroom. "What's going on?" asked the elderly man. "I thought I heard voices."

Chester smiled, his eyes livid with excitement. "You did," he replied. He held the wooden horse out to his grandfather. "I was told to give this to you … or, rather, to young Johnny."

With a trembling hand, Grandpa took the toy, his eyes brimming with youthful wonder. "So he finally made it," he said. "After all these years."

Chester watched as John McCorkendale gently cradled the wooden stallion with the reverence of some great and long sought after treasure. Then, limping, the old man returned to the comfort of his bed… and boyish dreams of decades long past.

2
A Soul's Wage

By Brian J. Hatcher

Sometimes, I wish I could find solace in melodrama. Maybe then I could let this thing go and move on. Convince myself that what happened to Derek wasn't my fault. Find a little comfort in a convenient little lie.

It began that day at Sullivan's. Sullivan's was, to us, the best bar in Baltimore. Not a private club, but it felt like one. Well-lit and nicely furnished, Sullivan's made a conscious effort to separate itself from the dive bars along the strip. There was no pool table or jukebox, and Sullivan's was neither a fight club nor a meat market. Just a quiet place to have a beer after work. Outside might be rain or snow, but inside the atmosphere was warm and the beers cold. It's where I first met Derek. We were kindred spirits, two small-town lads looking to make it in the big city, me from Kentucky and Derek from West Virginia. We had many good times at Sullivan's. It used to be the safest spot in the world. Now, I can't walk past the place.

I headed over to Sullivan's to relax after a hectic Thursday in early December. Terry, the owner, had the place decked out for Christmas. The 1951 black-and-white version of "Christmas Carol" played on the TV. Terry draped Christmas lights behind the bar, and he insisted every year on putting up a real Christmas tree. The smell of pine reminded me of home.

I found Derek at the bar. He already had our beers waiting. We downed them in a couple of gulps, to prime the pump. Terry brought us two fresh ones and tossed our empties. I waited until Derek took a sip and placed his bottle back on the counter before pulling the Royal Crown bag from my coat pocket. It jangled as I dropped it on the bar in front of him. "A little early, but anyway, Merry Christmas."

"Dude, what's this?" He untied the drawstrings and opened the bag. He dug out a few metal tokens and dropped them into his open palm, flipping them over with his fingers. "Where did you find these?"

"When I went to visit the folks for Thanksgiving. Granddad and a couple of my uncles used to collect coal scrip. My uncles lost interest after Granddad died and Dad wound up with the whole collection. He tossed them in a drawer and forgot about them. Since he didn't want them, I asked him if I could have them."

Derek pulled a few more pieces of scrip from the bag. "How much did he want?"

"Nothing. He just gave them to me."

"So you ripped off your Dad to get me a Christmas gift? I'm strangely touched."

"What do you mean?" I asked.

"Don't you know what they're worth?"

"Couldn't be that much."

"Au contraire," Derek said. "Scrip's a hot collector's item, long before I got into it. Most of these pieces are in pretty good shape. You'd get top dollar, especially for the West Virginia scrip."

"How much are we talking about?"

"About ten to fifty bucks apiece. There's probably three to four grand worth of scrip in this bag."

"Ouch."

Derek smiled. "Don't worry, I'll give you the money. Wouldn't want your Dad to kill you, and it's not like I can't afford it."

"That's right." I picked up my beer for a toast. "To your promotion."

We clinked our bottles together. "And to many more."

I let the last sip of beer warm in my mouth, savoring the taste, before I swallowed it. My mounting beer buzz did little to improve my mood. "I wish you'd send a little luck my way. Middle management is starting to get to me."

"Luck's got nothing to do with it."

"Maybe for you, but life's different for us mere mortals."

Derek took another swig of beer. He was about to put it down but paused, as if deciding something. "Preston, can I be honest with you?"

"Always."

Derek took one more drink before putting the bottle down. "Praying that upper management notices you won't get you anywhere. Stand around waiting for your ship to come in, and you'll starve to death on the dock."

"I'm not waiting around for anything. Every time a position comes up I'm the first to apply."

"C'mon, you know job postings are a formality," Derek said. "By the time you've seen them, management's already handpicked someone for the job."

"I know that. I apply so upper management sees I'm looking to move up. For all the good that's doing me."

"So no one's getting promoted?"

"A member of my team did, last month. Kid's just out of college. I trained him myself. But he gets bumped up and I stay right where I am."

"So do what he did."

"Not on your life. He's nothing but a toady. You couldn't get a good day's work out of the guy, but because he plays politics and knows somebody who knows somebody, he gets a break. I'm better than that. I'll get ahead, but I'll do it the right way."

"What exactly is the right way?"

"I have to tell you?"

Derek shook his head. "And that's your problem."

"What're you talking about?"

"It's called the American Dream," Derek said, "because you're dreaming if you think that works for anybody. That's just the carrot dangling in front of you to keep you on the treadmill."

"I get more work done than anyone in my department. Doesn't it make sense that I could accomplish even more if I'm given the chance?"

"Do you make someone the manager at Burger King because he's good at fries? It's apples and oranges. No knock on you, but any college grad could learn your job in six months. You're not going to impress upper management that way."

"Then what am I supposed to do?"

"That guy who got promoted," Derek asked, "ever see him?"

"Yeah. He comes around occasionally to talk to my supervisor. I found out he's handling my performance evaluation next period."

"Can't stand him, can you?"

"The little punk walks around like he's better than everyone else."

"Better than you, you mean. Afraid he's right?"

Derek got the reaction from me that, I'm sure, he wanted. "I'm better than he'll ever hope to be."

"Then prove it. You should send that man a card because he just gave you the best Christmas gift you've ever received. He showed you how to get ahead."

"And I suppose that's how you got your promotion," I said.

"I thought that was obvious."

"Yeah, whatever."

"You don't believe me?"

"You, a corporate suck-up? You're better than that."

"Get real, Preston. It's just part of the game. Everyone plays whether they want to or not, and if you're not winning, you're losing. Maybe it's not fair, but what is? Look at you. You're trying to get a position where you work less and get paid more. Is that fair?"

"It's not like that," I said.

"Go ahead, pull the other one. Look, there is always going to be a select few riding along on the backs of the masses dumb enough to let them. Take my bank, for example. We're about to cut Christmas bonuses, except for upper management's. Part of mine's going to pay for your Dad's coal scrip. That's not fair. But it's going to happen anyway."

"Why?"

"You know how the economy is right now. Everyone's cutting corners. Better that than layoffs."

"No, I mean why do you get to keep your bonuses?"

"R.H.I.P.," Derek said. "Rank Has Its Privileges."

"Aren't your employees going to get upset?"

"They might grumble but they won't say anything. Maybe someone'll quit, but they're in for a shock if they think it'll be different somewhere else."

"That doesn't make it right."

"Preston, there's no Santa Claus to give you everything you want for Christmas just because you've been good. Thought you knew that by now. This is the real world, and if you're not the hammer, you're the nail. Aren't you tired of being used? Then learn to be the user, because there are no other choices."

Terry brought our last round, which we drank in silence. Finally, Derek asked, "You mad at me?"

"No," I said. "I'm mad at somebody. I'm just not sure who."

"I wish life *was* fair, for everyone's sake. But there's nothing noble about pretending that it is. Dog-eat-dog doesn't begin to describe what life's really about. I've learned to accept that, but that doesn't change who I am. I did what I had to do to get ahead, that's all. It's just work."

"I don't know. If that's what it takes, I'm not sure it's worth it."

"You know my Grandpa worked in the mines?"

"For Brownie Gibraltar, yes, you told me."

"You ever see a man die from black lung? Grandpa, gasping for breath on his deathbed, was my first memory of him. The mining company paid my Grandfather in scrip and got rich while he contracted black lung and died poor. That's why I collect coal scrip, as a reminder. You know why they sent children into the mines to pull out the coal carts instead of using mules? Because it was too dangerous. It was easier to send another child into the mines than pay to replace a mule killed in a cave-in. Maybe the stakes aren't as high for us, but they're not that different. You're either feeding the machine, or the machine feeds you."

"Yeah, maybe."

Derek put his hand on my shoulder. "I know you have what it takes to make upper management. I wouldn't have said all this to you if I didn't think so. But you have to be willing to pay the price. Your choice. You don't have to play the game. Just have to settle for less. But I don't think you can." Derek pulled his wallet out. "Beer's on me tonight."

"Generous to a fault. You realize you're still going to have three ghosts visiting your house this Christmas, right?"

Derek laughed. "They better send more than three."

*　　*　　*

I didn't find Derek's brand of corporate nihilism appealing, but I couldn't argue his logic. I still can't. But, he could've kept quiet about how much

Dad's scrip was worth, so maybe he wasn't as mercenary as some would like to believe. But after the incident at the bank, I wondered if I ever really knew him at all.

Everyone wrote Derek off as a petty bureaucrat who got what he deserved, but that explanation couldn't satisfy me. Self-preservation alone should have been enough to stop him. Derek simply had no good reason to do what they said he did.

Most of what I know, I learned from secondhand accounts. The employees at Derek's bank received the bad news about their Christmas bonuses in a mass e-mail. They were none too thrilled, but that was nothing compared to how they felt when they received small manila envelopes through interdepartmental mail. Coin envelopes marked, "Xmas Bonus", each with a piece of coal scrip inside. I assume the majority of the scrip came from the Royal Crown bag I gave Derek. He must have dipped into his personal collection for the rest. Hot collector's item aside, no one appreciated the gesture. I don't know how much discussion and capitulation it took to keep the situation from getting uglier than it did, but when the smoke cleared, the bank fired Derek and he dropped out of sight.

I wanted to talk to him, find out what happened. He wouldn't answer his phone and, passing by his house, I never saw the lights on. He stopped coming by Sullivan's, and I couldn't blame him. I decided to give him time. Maybe I should have knocked on his door, checked up on him, but I didn't want to press the issue. I wish I had. By the time I did eventually stop by his place, he had long since left.

I wouldn't hear from him or see him again for almost a year.

* * *

Every December I volunteer at the soup kitchen the Unitarian Church sets up around Christmastime. Before someone mistakes me for a humanitarian, I should say I started doing it because someone stopped me at church and I couldn't come up with an excuse quickly enough. I don't look forward to it. Standing next to those homeless men, you see and smell things you don't want to know about. But I should also say that, once I get into the swing of things, it's not that bad.

Two days before Christmas, as I scooped mashed potatoes onto waiting plates, someone halfway down the food line stepped out and headed toward the door, because he'd seen me. I didn't get a good look at him but I slid out from behind the counter and went after him. I'm not sure why. I didn't exactly recognize him but I thought I knew him. I'm not claiming psychic powers, but if someone were to ask me why I went after him, how I knew, I'd still give the same answer: *Who else could it be?*

I followed him outside. He picked up his pace to put some distance between us.

"Derek, wait."

He stopped, but didn't turn around. His head slumped. Once he realized I knew him, I guess he figured he had no dignity left to save.

The dirty tan overcoat and tattered wool toboggan pulled over his head couldn't have kept him very warm. His hacking cough proved it. I could feel the weight around him that bent his shoulders down. Everything about him seemed frail and broken.

Derek started to speak, but a coughing fit stopped him. He finally managed to catch his breath. "I didn't expect to see you here."

"You know I work the soup kitchen."

"Back in Baltimore. Didn't realize you'd taken your show on the road."

"Derek," I said, "this is Baltimore."

It took a moment for him to believe me. "Huh? Guess I got lost."

"Where were you?"

I waited for another coughing fit to pass before he answered. "A little bit of every place I guess. Wound up in a homeless shelter in Charleston, West Virginia. People are always stealing from you so I kept outdoors for a while. Slept in Davis Square with a couple of guys. We looked out for each other. When the weather turned cold, we decided to head south. We were separated. Don't know how long I've been walking."

"How did this happen? I knew things would be tough for you, but you're a smart guy. You could get a job anywhere. Even fast food would be better than this."

"They knew my pride wouldn't let me. By the time I was desperate enough to do anything, I'd fallen too far. They thought of everything."

"Who did?" I asked.

"Humanity is tenuous, fickle thing. No one is ever farther than one step from the gutter. One moment of weakness and you're cast down. I was so busy looking up, I didn't realize how far down the bottom could go."

"Why did you do it?" I asked. "What did you think mailing that scrip would get you?"

"Do you know what coal scrip really is?"

"What?"

"It's life and death. It's a man's soul pressed into a cheap piece of metal. It's nothing and everything."

"Yes, I know, and it's a hot collector's item. Why did you do it?"

"Didn't you hear me? Every piece of scrip is a man's soul. Deeper than blood. I held them in my hands. Hundreds of men's souls." Something made him shiver besides the cold. "I'm not a monster. What right do they have to judge me? I only wanted to make something of myself. What gives them the right? I had everything, and they were nothing. Just souls for me to hold in my hands. What happened to them, it wasn't my fault."

Derek swayed like a ghost draped in skin. Had he appeared to me as a spirit covered in chains, lockboxes, and ledger books, he couldn't have frightened me more that he did at that moment.

I realized I didn't have my coat on. "Let's get out of the cold." I took him by one greasy sleeve and led him inside, got him a cup of coffee that he barely touched, and then called an ambulance.

I'd hoped to ruin the story. Something anticlimactic, like Derek cleaning up and getting his life back on track. Pneumonia forced the ridiculous, predictable ending. I paid for the funeral.

I wish I could find solace in melodrama. I'll never know what happened to Derek, or who really sent the coal scrip. I'm not sure I want to. Derek said it would take more than three ghosts to bring him down. Several hundred, I'd say, would be more than enough to do the trick.

If there were some moral to this story, some reason I could understand— but there is no moral. It's not about how a man's ambition eventually destroyed him. There are others like Derek and worse, their karmic debts left suspiciously unpaid. And it's no object lesson for me. I don't think of myself, nor have I ever been mistaken for, the Center of the Universe. There's nothing I need to learn that a man should die to teach me. So there is no tidy ending.

I have only this for a coda.

On my dresser at home sits a five-dollar scrip I took out of the Royal Crown bag before I gave it to Derek. Stamped from brass and steel, it says "Brownie Gibraltar", the mine Derek's grandfather worked for. I planned to have it framed or shadowboxed or something. I should throw it away. I still might. But right now, I can't. I look at that token, almost every day, and for some reason I don't want to think about it, it terrifies me more than anything I've ever known.

19

3
Lorelei Wakes At Midnight

By Patricia Hughes

The moment I saw it, the dulcimer cast its spell. Glistening walnut, delicately carved in a twisting leaf pattern, bespoke skill.

"Craftsmanship." The wrinkled shopkeeper handed me the instrument. "Try it if you like, young man."

I ran my hand over the curve of the hourglass shape. Rich tones resonated through the room when I strummed the strings. "I'm just an amateur. I'd like to hear it played by someone who knows what he's doing."

"Can't play. Just run the shop."

"Lorelei wakes at midnight," said a stooped old woman near the counter. "She sings and plays 'til dawn."

"Hush, Hattie." To me he said, "These hills are full of superstition."

"Superstition?" Her eyes narrowed. "Then, sell 'im the thing."

"How much is it?" I asked.

"Not for sale. Been in my family for generations. It was handcrafted by a young mountain woman. Sold several times before my great great grandfather bought it. It'll pass to my son when I'm gone."

"I wouldn't part with it either."

The shopkeeper hung the dulcimer back on the wall. "Is there something else I can help you with?"

I bought a few trinkets then took a room at the inn across from the shop. I went to sleep thinking of the dulcimer. My dreams filled with the haunting, distant song of a young woman playing flawlessly on the antique dulcimer. I awoke wishing it had been real.

In the months that followed I would take an occasional weekend and drive to the little shop in the mountains, just to stand around staring at the dulcimer. I would stay at the inn and dream about its music. I finally told myself I must come to my senses. I had better things to do than obsess over an antique dulcimer I could never own.

I stayed away for several months. Then, just before Christmas, I decided to make one last trip. There was a middle-aged man running the shop. When I inquired about the old shopkeeper, he replied, "Heart attack. I'm his son, Tom Dade."

"I'm sorry."

"I'm just wrapping things up. House is sold. I'm sleeping in the back room of the shop tonight. I've lined up a buyer for this place, too. I'll be out of here soon."

"Ye're a fool." The same old woman I'd seen that first day stood in the doorway.

"You're the fool," snapped Dade, "believing such superstitious nonsense."

"We'll see soon enough which of us is the fool, Tom Dade."

The exchange made me uncomfortable. But if Dade was keeping neither house nor shop, perhaps he wasn't as sentimental as his father. I seized the moment. "How much is the dulcimer on the wall?"

"Ye'll regret it," said the old woman.

Dade glared at her. "It's not marked, but I think we can come to an agreement."

After a bit of haggling, I left thinking I had the better of the bargain.

"Ya should've listened," said the old woman. "Lorelei is 'specially restless 'round Christmas."

* * *

That night, I awakened from a dreamless sleep when the frantic screams of a woman filled my room. My heart pounding, I jumped out of bed then froze. I listened.

Silence.

I switched on the light. The room was empty, although I would have sworn the screams originated right beside me. I grabbed my robe and peeked out in the hall. I saw nothing except other guests standing in their doorways.

"What was that?" The woman across the hall was trembling.

"I didn't hear anything," said her husband.

"It sounded like someone being murdered," said a man two doors down.

Some people had heard the screams; others had not. Those not awakened by the screams were roused by the proprietor as he checked all the rooms at the insistence of the woman across the hall. Nothing was amiss. I retreated to my room and looked out the window. The street was dark and quiet.

I picked up the mystery novel I had been reading then tossed it aside. The last thing I wanted to contemplate at that moment was a murder. My eyes fell on the dulcimer. I strummed a chord.

Suddenly, I heard screaming again—masculine screams from outside the inn. I drew back the curtains. Across the street, flames leapt from the shop's windows. I reached for my cell. No service.

I ran from my room. "Get some help!" I shouted to the proprietor.

The screams continued. Smoke billowed from the shop. I tried the door.

Locked.

I kicked four times before it opened. A blast of heat hit my face. I jumped back just in time to avoid the flames. The screams stopped. Despite the heat from the flames, a chill shuddered through my body.

Sirens wailed as one fire truck and a number of pickups rushed through the narrow streets to fight the fire. Firemen and volunteers worked frantically; but in the end, the shop collapsed into a mound of smoldering rubble. The first rays of dawn peeped over the mountains as they placed Dade's remains into a body bag.

"I warned 'im." The old woman appeared beside me. "I warned ye, too." She turned and hobbled off.

"Wait." I hurried to catch her. "What exactly are you warning me about?"

"Lorelei wakes at midnight." She stopped in front of a small, clapboard house. "Ya won't believe me..." She opened the door. "...yet." She shuffled through the door then turned. "Most times ya can find me here. Don't sell the dulcimer and don't give it away." She closed the door in my face.

*   *   *

I loaded my bag and the dulcimer into my car and headed for the city. After the previous night's experience I doubted I would ever venture back to the little town. On the bright side, the dulcimer I had coveted so long was mine. Or was it the bright side? I couldn't get the old woman's warning out of my mind. I chastised myself. What had happened to Dade was a cruel coincidence, or else the old woman had set the fire herself.

Once home, I collapsed into bed and was asleep in no time. I dreamed an angelic voice accompanied by the melodious tones of the dulcimer. Gradually I realized I was not dreaming. I opened my eyes. Swathed in moonlight, a young woman, poorly dressed in a long skirt many times mended, was playing my dulcimer and singing. Auburn locks cascaded down her back. Her face was not beautiful but was in its own way compelling.

I flipped on the light. "How did you get in here?"

She blinked and stopped playing.

I thought about the baseball bat under my bed. Just because she was a woman, didn't mean she couldn't be dangerous. "Who are you?" I asked.

"Lorelei."

The sound of the name nearly stopped my heart. Surely, I was dreaming, after all. I glanced at the clock. It was just after midnight.

"What are you doing here?" I managed after a moment.

She looked at me as if I had asked a stupid question. "Singin'." She ran her fingers along the curve of the dulcimer. "I made it myself."

I remembered the old shopkeeper had said a young mountain woman had made the dulcimer. But that was in the days of his great great grandfather.

She looked at me coyly. "Ya like my dulcimer, don't ya?"

"Very much," I answered when I found my voice.

"It took a long time in the makin'. Ya know, each piece o' wood is different, even pieces from the same tree. Ya have to test 'em. Some pieces vibrate long and loud when ya strike 'em. They sing, while others are dull, their sound dyin' quickly." She strummed the dulcimer. "Hear that? I chose walnut over cherry wood. The sound is sweeter, more mellow." She strummed another chord.

"Ya do like my dulcimer, don't ya?" She gazed at me with hypnotic eyes. "Ya wouldn't sell it, would ya?"

"Uh…" I stammered. The old woman's warning echoed in my mind. "No… I, ah… No."

I got little sleep that night, or the next four nights either. It was just like the old woman said. Lorelei wakes at midnight. She sings and plays 'til dawn.

I became exhausted. Hearing sweet music at a distance was one thing.

24

Having a singing ghost a few feet away from you is entirely another. Despite it all, I would doze, but my sleep was not restful. Not even the few hours I could catch between work and midnight were restful. I was worried the neighbors would start to complain. Fortunately, my closest neighbors were gone for the holidays.

At work my productivity became zilch. I made errors. My superiors were eyeing me strangely. Some of my co-workers were becoming conciliatory, while that devious Patterson was grinning like a Cheshire cat. He'd had his eye on my job for a long time.

Friday, after work, I picked up the dulcimer and headed back to the village. Three times I nodded off and nearly went off the road. I pulled over and slept until midnight when Lorelei's song awakened me.

Bright and early Saturday morning, I was on the old woman's doorstep. "Knew ye'd be back," she said, as she let me in.

The interior was rustic, simple, and sparsely furnished. I sat on a lumpy couch covered with a handmade quilt that would have been the envy of every woman I know.

"Tell me about Lorelei," I said.

The old woman grinned. One of her front teeth was missing; the others, stained. A lump of chewing tobacco bulged behind her cheek. "Seen her, have ya?"

"Every night, just like you said, between midnight and dawn."

"Warned ya, I did."

"Yes, you did; but I didn't understand."

"Ya didn't want to," she said. "All o' ya with yer fancy cars and clothes and big jobs in the big cities... Ya think ya know it all. But ya don't."

"Tell me about Lorelei," I repeated. "Please."

The old woman spat into an empty coffee can. "A mountain girl, she

25

was, poor as dirt. Didn't have nuthin' 'cept a talent for music she got from her dead pa. Lived with her ma in a fallin' down shack, just the two of 'em. Worked from morn 'til night just to make ends meet.

"Lorelei wanted somethin' beautiful. She made the dulcimer. Worked on it instead of sleepin'. Went without food to buy what little she needed that she couldn't get from the woods. When she was done, it was a beauty. She'd sing and play that thing half the night. It was the only bit o' happiness that girl ever had.

"Then one day, she come home and the dulcimer was gone. Her ma had sold it to the owner of the mines. Nobody knows exactly what happened that night, but the next mornin' folks found Lorelei froze to death in a snowdrift beside the Cooper house. When they went to tell her ma, they found what was left of her burnt up in the ashes of the shack.

"Cooper had bought the dulcimer as a Christmas present for his daughter. But in no time at all, he sold it to a man named McNeil. The night he sold it, Cooper's big house burned to the ground. Cooper and all his family perished. Afore long, McNeil sold the dulcimer, and he burnt up, too. The next owner just gave it away, but he burnt anyway. Finally, it got sold to Lucas Dade. Ol' Luke was dumb enough to buy it, but smart enough to figure out what was goin' on. After he lost enough sleep, he built the shop and hung the dulcimer on the wall to be admired. Lorelei liked that, she did. And Ol' Luke and his sons after him got to sleep nights away from the shop. Worked fine 'til Tom Dade decided he knew mor'n his forebears."

"Are you saying there's no way for me to get rid of this thing?" I asked.

"Not if'n ya don't want to be a cinder." The old woman spat again. "Lorelei likes her work to be appreciated."

I left the old woman and walked back to the inn. I was shaken, but exhausted enough that I slept like the dead until Lorelei woke me at midnight.

Her song painted the mountains as she had known them, both beautiful and harsh. I listened until I gathered enough courage to ask. "What happened when your mother sold the dulcimer?"

Lorelei's eyes glowed red. "She had no right! It was mine! I made it. It was the only purty thing I ever owned. She had no right!"

My chest tightened. I felt clammy. I didn't want her angry. "You're right, Lorelei. She shouldn't have sold it."

Lorelei seemed pacified.

"But why did she sell it?" I asked.

"She said to buy food—something special for Christmas. I sacrificed to make it. She had no right. I told her so." Lorelei straightened and hovered a few inches off the floor. "I grabbed the crock she had the money in. She grabbed too. She slapped me. I slapped her back. We fought 'til we fell and the crock broke. She slapped me again, and I pushed her. She fell 'gainst the table and knocked over the lantern. Her skirt caught fire."

Lorelei paused. Her image became translucent. "Ma hollered and hollered, but all I could think of was the dulcimer. I gathered the money and ran. I hurried so, I didn't even grab my shawl. I ran all the way to the Big House.

"The Coopers were havin' a party. There was lots o' holly and red ribbon and a big tree lit with candles and presents 'neath it. I tried to tell 'em the dulcimer was mine. I tried to give the money back. Nobody listened. They slammed the door in my face.

"I didn't know what to do. I couldn't go home. Ma was awful mad. I sat down and cried. It was snowin', cold. I guess I just went to sleep where I was.

"When I woke up, I went into Mr. Cooper's House. This time I didn't have no trouble gettin' in."

This time you were dead, I realized. I shivered.

"I saw the dulcimer and picked it up. I tried to leave the money, but I couldn't find it. My pockets were empty. I couldn't get the dulcimer through the door."

Of course not. It's a solid object. I tried to swallow. My throat was dry.

"I s'pose in a way it belonged to Mr. Cooper. Ma sold it to 'im, even though she had no right. But it was mine, too. So, I played it." She strummed a few chords.

"Mr. Cooper didn't like my playin'. He told me to leave, but he didn't seem to be able to throw me out anymore. So, I didn't let it fret me none. Ever' night I play." Lorelei strummed a few more chords. Her image became more opaque.

"Lorelei, what happened when Mr. Cooper sold the dulcimer?"

Lorelei's eyes sparked red again. "He had no right. I'm the only one who has that right. I told him so. Then, just like Ma, he started to burn, even though there was no lantern."

My blood turned to ice. Lorelei began to sing.

What was I going to do? Lorelei was not only a ghost, she was insane. The future spread before me in an endless array of sleepless nights and haunting melodies. I had difficulty seeing myself as a mountain shopkeeper, although it might be worth trying. Maybe I could get a night job and sleep days. So much for an up and coming career. I pictured Patterson's grin as he took over my office. There had to be a better way. Rick Patterson was not going to profit at my expense.

Lorelei played, while I thought of one useless plan after another. Then, the old woman's words drifted through my mind. Lorelei had accepted the shop because Lorelei likes her work to be appreciated. Perhaps there was a way.

"It's a shame about the shop, isn't it?" I said.

Lorelei glared. "He sold my dulcimer."

"I didn't mean Tom Dade." Perspiration began to bead on my forehead. "I meant the shop itself. People could come into the shop and see what a magnificent instrument you made. Now that the shop's gone, they can't do that anymore."

Lorelei's voice was soft, almost seductive. "Ya like my dulcimer, don't ya?"

"Very much. That's why I came so often to see it. That's why I bought it." I was quick to add, "I would never part with it." I paused. "But should I be the only one who can appreciate its beauty?"

*   *   *

Rick Patterson finally got my job. I've been promoted. I'm Patterson's supervisor. My plans include a long, illustrious career and a long, happy life. But just in case I should meet with an untimely end, I've made a will. I'm leaving the dulcimer to Patterson.

Ah, yes… The dulcimer. There it is, once more hanging on a wall, very much like I first saw it. Despite its terror, it still fascinates me—it and Lorelei. Occasionally, I miss hearing her sing. Then, I come to my senses.

As I gaze at the dulcimer, I realize Mr. Jamison, the curator, is standing beside me. "Beautiful," he says, "just beautiful. We really appreciate your lending it to the museum. It's such an exquisite example of the sophistication of some of the mountain crafts." He pauses. "Are you certain you won't consider selling it to us?"

"Quite certain." I've made sure Lorelei understands I still own the dulcimer, and I visit often—especially around Christmas. "However, you may display it as long as you like."

"Well," he sighs. "I'd best get back to those applications. Surely, someone will have some longevity."

"Is there a problem?"

"Yes. We just can't seem to keep security guards on our night shift. I just don't understand it."

I do, I think as I take another look at the glistening walnut finish, the carefully carved sound holes. *Lorelei wakes at midnight.*

4

A Sky Full of Stars and a Big Green Forever

By Steve Vernon

I wish I was anywhere but Christmas.

Winter hung over the Alleghenies like a promise waiting to be kept. Stars winked down, a hoot owl tolled the hour in low barrelled tones, and I was thinking about my Dad.

It had been a year since he'd let go just last Christmas. He'd tried to walk past the Yule but the paper thin walls of a heart that had been broken by my mother's death a year before had torn open and let go.

Are you doing the math? That's two Christmases and two deaths of people more nearer than hope to me.

So don't talk to me about celebration.

Things fall away in this life. Everything you try to hang on to is made of wind and smoke and a slippery grip. I've left so much behind me on this road from womb to tomb—a marriage, kids who never call, and the lingering bitter aftertaste of a world gone gray, full of unfulfilled dreams.

I'm not complaining, you understand. We get our share and keep some and give some back and some just walks away but a body is bound to wonder, sometimes. It's as natural as what we borrow with every hard-took breath.

It will be Christmas tomorrow and I have sent a few cards and filled an old gray work sock with a bone and a chew toy for my bulldog Moose who even now is wagging the memory of his tail at me and happily slobbering on the rug.

That's something, I guess.

If you don't count Moose then I am completely alone, a condition I'm slowly growing used to. I'm sitting here by the hearth, listening to the flames talking smack with the pine kindling, and chunks of oak I've fed it.

Firewood always reminds me of a riddle Dad used to tell.

"If pine burns so fast and oak so long and strong, how has the evergreen ever learned to last?"

There wasn't any answer, of course. It was just a way that Dad had of making every minute last a little longer than it was built for. He had a way of slowing time down and making it sit and grin.

He made me grin, too.

Lord, how I miss the man.

I can see him now, sorting through the woodpile, the whorls and callous of his fingertips looking hard at every chunk he'd pick up. He had a way of hefting each stick of wood as if he was weighing its worth. He never lingered, it was a smooth and natural process, but each piece of timber had to pass that test.

I'm not saying he was a fussy man, but he could be awfully particular when he wanted to be. It paid off when he courted my mother.

"I caught her eye in high school," he'd told me. "But she went and married the quarterback on our football team. He showed her his bad side, shortly after the honeymoon. She stayed with him for six years, through black and blue, until he died choking on a fist full of salted nuts, over a warm beer and a bad joke."

I can still see Dad smiling over that last remark, not out of spite but just savouring the irony. He told the story the same way every time he was asked to, which was how I knew that it was a little more than just a story. After he'd given

32

her a chance to mourn what she'd lost, my Dad courted my mother with the intensity of a flame that's been kindling for a lot of long years. Every day he'd bring her bunches of wild roses and sweet-smelling daisies and fistfuls of blue forget-me-not flowers.

You see, my Dad never did have much in the way of folding money, so he learned to make do with another kind of green.

The kind of green that lasted.

In the years that I shared with them I have never seen the man utter a cross word or raise a hand of anger towards my mother. He cherished her with every breath he took. He worked at the wood mill, pushing boards through a sharp whirling saw blade, singing a quiet hosanna of thankfulness to every speck of sawdust and sweat that flew by his ears.

He never missed her birthday. He never forgot to leave the coffee pot brewing before he left for work. I can see him even now, through the dusty looking glass of memory, that old fedora perched on his head, a bright green feather stabbed through the hat band. That long loping way he'd walk that always made me feel like he would never stop moving.

Christmas was his favourite time of year. I can remember when he'd put the window lights on and Momma would always say that he had hung the stars in the night sky—like that string of five and dime lights glinting through the icicles and frosted pane was anything more than a simple pleasure.

Yes sir, my Dad did Christmas up right. Every winter he'd pull on a pair of snowshoes and he'd haul that old sled of his out to the back field where he'd search for hours until he found the proper Christmas tree. Somehow it just wouldn't be Christmas for Dad without that long cold walk through the snow, pushing the ghost of his breath forward into the crisp morning air.

When I got older he'd let me tag along. Well, actually he'd tell me to tag along. In fact, now that I think of it he sort of dragged me everywhere I had to go to.

It was on my third tag-along-drag that he first told me the story.

I was complaining at the time. Back then I was good at complaining. Being as young as I was I did an awful lot of complaining about things that couldn't ever be changed.

"What do we need an old Christmas tree for anyway?" I asked. "Why don't we just buy one at the lot downtown?"

Dad just kept on walking, moving those snowshoes through the snow like he was fixing to hike to Alaska.

"Leaves and needles grow on trees," he told me. "Not money."

"If we bought ourselves an artificial tree we could stay inside and keep warm. They last forever."

He looked at me like I was seven kinds of stupid. Not in a mean way, just in a Dad kind of way.

Even then I knew the difference.

"If that's what you call lasting," he said. "I'll settle for what comes first."

I had to bite.

"So what comes first?" I asked.

"What's real, that's what comes first," Dad said. "Something that you can believe in is what you want to have and hold on to."

"Try holding on to a tree and all you'll catch is splinters," I pointed out.

I wasn't trying to be smart. I just sounded that way, because I was awfully young, but Dad knew the difference, too.

"Trees are special," he said. "And pine and fir trees are even more special. They keep green all winter for a reason."

"That's because they're conifers," I said. "I learned that in school."

"You learn a lot of things in school," Dad said. "Some are more important than others."

"So why do they keep green?"

"They keep green because they've been blessed," Dad said. "See them moving on the sky-line? The way they lean and sway in the wind? The old folk called them heaven painters. I just call them masterpieces."

"Well maybe we could get them to paint the house next summer, instead of me and you," I said.

Dad just looked me like I had discovered an eighth kind of stupidity.

"The evergreen is blessed," he said. "Back in Bethlehem when the baby child was born the old king-trees all crowded around the stable to have a look and they pushed the little evergreen out of the way. The olive tree brought fat green olives and the palm tree brought dates but the little evergreen had nothing until the Christmas angel looked down and dropped a few stars from heaven on the evergreen's boughs. The baby Jesus looked up and saw those stars all bright and shiny on those thickety green-whiskered branches and he up and laughed. So every winter, when the nights are as dark and long as you think they could ever get you look at the green promise of the Christmas tree, with the stars hung on the branches and everything just feels better."

"So why do we have to feel better way the heck out here in the winter cold?" I asked.

"Because it's out here, in the snow and the cold where you can hear the sound of the wind blowing and rattling through the needles of the evergreen—well, that's just the sound of the Christ child laughing at the blow of the cold."

The story had sounded like horse feathers and hogwash back then and it still did even now. All those windy old stories aside, I missed my Dad and I missed my Mom. I know you aren't supposed to be so silly—a man at fifty and all—but I missed them and it left a kind of lonely hole in my heart that I didn't believe could ever get full.

Yup, merry frozen Christmas, you bet.

What did I have to celebrate for?

I remembered two Christmases ago, when the cancer took Mom. I remember the beautiful woman with the soft girlish laugh, worn away to nothing more than a scarecrow. Dad kept watch by her bedside through the whole time, telling her jokes and stories to make her smile.

Then, after she passed away Dad stopped talking. He stopped even laughing. That was the year he stopped going to the saw mill. He wouldn't even bother getting dressed. He just wore that old plaid housecoat that Momma gave him the Christmas before.

Moped around the house, stared out the window, and waited.

Then, the week before Christmas I got up to the smell of smoke. I went down to the living room and found my father there, on his knees before the fireplace hearth, burning that smelly old housecoat. He was crying and laughing at the same time, like he was glad to let go of that load he'd been carrying in silence the whole year long.

I just sat there for a while on the couch, looking at the bent back of the man who had taught me how to grow and stand tall, crouched now in the sorrow of having to let go.

"I'm going to walk past Christmas," he told me. "I don't want you to see the holiday as a time of mourning. We'll cut ourselves a tree and wrap a few presents and I'll hang the stars in the window. Then, come the new year, I'll walk a little further to where your Momma is waiting for me."

Only he didn't.

Couldn't, I guess.

First time I ever remember Dad not keeping a promise.

He tiptoed up to Christmas's door and on the night before Christmas he gave up the ghost.

Scrooge had three of them.

Dad, only one.

So I'm sitting here, waiting for the holiday to pass so that I can get back to my work and lose myself in the tedium of toil.

"I hate Christmas," I said to Moose, who only let his tongue hang out a little closer to the floorboards.

I heard a banging at the door, like boots coming up the porch stairs. Something heavy being dropped.

"Now what?"

Just then, the house lights went out.

Darn this old shack.

Now I have to go and change the fuse.

The banging on the door got a little louder. It sounded like scratching, like a half a thousand cats were at the door trying to claw their way in.

Old Moose barked happily.

Stupid dog.

I fumbled in the darkness until I found the flashlight.

I walked to the door, shining the flashlight before me.

Old Moose, he just kept wagging that sawed-off stump of a tail like he was trying to give birth to the ghost of Chubby Checker.

I don't know why I felt frightened. Maybe it was the dark, maybe it was the lonely, maybe I was just scared that Old Moose was going to wag what was left of his tail away.

"Who is it?" I asked softly, clearing my throat.

No answer.

I opened the door slowly.

The hinges creaked like they had never heard of WD-40.

I looked outside and smelled pine.

There standing at the doorway was a freshly cut Christmas tree. The light of my flashlight reflected prettily off the icicles dangling from the branches.

I walked out into the yard, tiptoeing softly past the Christmas tree leaned against the front door.

It began to snow.

In the distance I heard the sound of snowshoes chuffing and stepping somewhere beyond the darkness.

I felt the snow upon my cheekbone, soft and wet and sweet as a mother's goodbye kiss.

"Nice tree, Dad."

And right then and right there I was glad to be standing in the darkness, deep within the silent heart of Christmas. I knew where Dad kept the string of Christmas lights and I figured I could have them shining like a kite string of stars in the window long before the sun rose up and remembered how to smile.

5

The Christmas Bane

By S. Clayton Rhodes

Lefty Bohach lay on his back staring at the empty bunk above him, wishing for a smoke.

The only thing breaking the silence was the scuff of footsteps coming down the short hallway.

"How ya doin', Myron?" Beyond the cream-painted bars Carbon Hill's Chief of Police, Dalton Strecker, pulled up a chair. The grate of wooden legs on tile was like nails on a chalkboard.

"Name's Lefty," Bohach corrected.

"Oh, yeah. *Lefty*. Tough guy like you, course you gotta have a good, strong name."

"'S'right," Lefty agreed, hoping the cop was finished but somehow knowing he wasn't.

Strecker leaned forward. "Tell me something, Bohach, you ever consider another line of work?"

Sensing this wasn't going to end any time soon, Lefty sat up and gulped from the mostly cold cup of coffee from the sink edge.

"See, I been lookin' at your record. Printed out your whole life story." Strecker snapped the manila file with the back of one hand. "Every convenience store you knocked over, every car you heisted, all the times you were picked up for possession, it's all here."

"I'm sure there's a point to this."

"Sure. The point is sewer water always runs deep." The cop let loose a laugh every bit as grating as the scraping chair legs had been a moment before. "Seriously, though, this file. . . it paints a picture. It says, 'Strecker, this here's one hapless crook who couldn't do worse if he tried.'"

An understatement if ever there was one, Lefty had to admit. He'd been passing through town this morning and what should happen but they stopped him for a busted brake light, of all things. When the patrolman called in, dispatch ran a routine check and learned Lefty was wanted for a whole slew of misdemeanors. These were in addition, of course, to the two counts of armed robbery. He was promptly put on ice until he could be transferred after the holiday.

"If it's any consolation," Strecker went on, "they'da nabbed you sooner or later if not here. Guys like you always trip up."

Lefty pretended to inspect a hangnail. Maybe if he continued acting bored, Strecker would eventually get the hint. No such luck. The cop kept yakking until Lefty finally lost it and told him to piss off.

"Easy, Tiger. Just making conversation. Still, I do hafta wonder. . . with all the times you've been caught, jailed, and let back out, did it ever cross your mind there could be an easier way to make a buck?"

In addition to getting under Lefty's skin, the cop had an uncanny talent for zeroing in on the sore spots. "I, I don't know how to do anything." Lefty instantly hated himself for showing any sign of weakness.

Strecker laughed again—that rattling, gut-busting laughter. "Well, isn't that the saddest thing? You can't learn to push a mop, so you fall into a life of crime.

Chowtime's in twenty, Slick. Have any special requests for your Christmas Eve dinner, seeing as how it may be your last?"

"Huh?"

"Never mind. I'll bring you something nice."

*　　　*　　　*

The "something nice" turned out to be a two-piece meal from KFC. The chicken was stringy, the biscuit dry. Lefty flushed the potatoes, which were as tasty as wallpaper paste, down the toilet.

Later, a little after ten o'clock, based on the bonging of the courthouse tower clock, Strecker returned. He snapped on the corridor lights and brought the chair close again.

Lefty squinted his eyes against the fluorescent glare. "What, are you bored or something, Chief? Why you keep pestering me?"

Strecker grinned. "Okay, I admit I mighta been a little hard on you earlier, but my point remains. Consider redeeming yourself, Bohach. Turn yourself around before it's too late."

"I'll agree to anything. Just lemme get some sleep, willya?"

Strecker ignored the comment, instead saying, "Ever hear of a fella by the name of Krampus?"

"Can't say that I have."

"Thought as much." The manila file with Lefty's rap sheet Strecker had held before had been replaced by a worn leather book, which the police chief slid through the bars. "Have yourself a looksee."

It was a scrapbook, and the spine cracked when Lefty opened it. Inside was a real treat. Beneath the protective sheeting were pages of postcards yellowed with age, colored prints, and sketches. And every image contained some form of devilish creature.

"That fella there," Strecker continued once Lefty had his initial glance, "is Krampus. Sometimes called Black Peter, Black Rupert, and a slew of other names."

Lefty continued leafing through. The cards were clearly Christmas in

41

nature but in each one the hairy demon was present. The interpretations varied, but on a few details all the artists were consistent. He had the hindquarters of a goat, a long tail, curving horns, and eyes shining like lamps. In most cases, he was threatening children or brandishing switches.

Strecker scratched a slack jaw then attempted an explanation. "I've been researching this guy for a while now. Not a lot to be found out, either. What I *have* gathered is that Christmas is a constantly evolving holiday. And more has been forgotten than has been kept. It began as a pagan celebration—this was before the church got involved. To get the unwashed masses on board with the idea of organized religion, the Church says, 'Okay, y'all can keep your winter solstice, so long as when you celebrate you honor the birthday of our Lord and Savior.' The Roman Catholics set it for December sixth, the day the real St. Nicholas died—the one who lived in Turkey, not the one shaking bells for The Salvation Army. The Protestants eventually moved things to the twenty-fifth. As for Krampus, some European traditions say he was St. Nicholas' dark servant, while others suggest they're flip sides of the same coin."

Lefty cleared his throat and said, "Look, Strecker, don't you have some place to be Christmas Eve?"

Again Strecker's face broke into a grin. "Kid, you may think this is some kinda funny, but I'm doing you a favor. Remember I said I was here about your redemption? We'll see if you have the brains to do the right thing once I'm done."

An ice storm had moved in an hour or so before, and sleet chattered at the thick glass and heavy-gauge mesh within the window overhead. Having seen enough of the book, Lefty passed it back through the bars.

Strecker flipped through the album, stopping at one particular page and turning it around for Lefty to see. "Look here. A perfect example of Krampus' relationship to Christmas."

In the picture an old-fashioned St. Nicholas, looking suitably bishop-like in his pointy hat and white robes and giving out sweet rolls to the penitent children. Meanwhile the decidedly evil-looking Krampus waited just outside the doorway for his turn at the not-so-good children cowering beneath a table. On another postcard, the demon had a wicker basket strapped to his back, and in the basket a distressed toddler thrashed. The ground beneath them gave way to a chasm of flames—presumably the way to hell.

Strecker offered Bohach a smoke and Lefty cupped the Camel tip to flame.

"You sure those pictures are legit?" Lefty wondered, waving out the single match. "I mean, how come I never heard anything about this Krampus 'til now?"

"The Christians of the late 1800s kept their kids in line with threats of Krampus coming for their souls. I suppose by and by folks got to thinking a devil coming to Christmas was unsettling for anyone's holiday, and he fell by the wayside. If you've ever heard about Santa Claus leaving switches instead of toys for the bad kids, it started here. A holdover from the Krampus days."

Lefty blew smoke at the bars. "I appreciate all this, Chief, don't think I don't. There's nothin' I like better than bein' woke up to hear some good ole-fashioned fairytales. But I just don't get it. First you say you're here about my redemption then you show me pictures of Satan's second cousin. What gives?"

Strecker smiled. "I did promise we'd talk about your salvation, Bohach, and we're almost there. Scout's honor." He held up two fingers. "Just stay with me a bit longer, okay?"

Lefty spread his hands and said around the cigarette, "I ain't goin' anywhere."

Strecker nodded. "As it happens, we got our own version of Krampus right here in Carbon Hill. Only we call him the Christmas Bane." He must have seen Lefty's eyebrows raise because he said, "That's right. You're probably thinking, 'Crazy old cop, now I *know* you've gone round the bend,' but it's true. Near as I can tell, he showed up in the late 1950s, 'bout the time the coalmine petered out. A widow woman was first to see him. Spied the old boy from her bedroom window one Christmas Eve, traipsing past her house going on midnight. He had, she said, eyes big as saucers and a head full o' teeth like fence pickets. Goat-hoof feet clomping through the snow, and a long, ratty tail whooshing behind him. Come morning, everyone learned some old geezer on Route 21 bought the farm. Then the widow spilled the beans on what she saw. Everyone thought her tree was a few apples short of a bushel, let me tell ya. Until the next Christmas, that is."

The chief went on to say how more people spotted the Christmas Bane over the years, and on each yuletide season since some hapless soul would be found dead in his bed, asphyxiated by a gas leak, or electrocuted from a freak mishap with the tree lights. Folks didn't know what he was or where he came from, but they got into the habit of putting out plates of food on their front stoops as sort of an offering. 'Eat this food and not my soul,' must have been the message they hoped to convey. According to Strecker, it must have worked, too. But the folks who had a black spot on their soul and didn't believe in the Christmas Bane, or left no offering. . . those were the folks who were likely to be singled out.

Lefty laughed a little. The police chief did spin an interesting yarn, and his Satanic scrapbook was a great visual aid. "And you figure this local bogey will set his sights on me tonight?"

Strecker didn't bat an eye. "I figure it's a good bet, and I suggest keeping an open mind on this. Could save your skin."

"All right," Lefty said. "If Krampus and your Christmas Bane are one and the same, where's he been between the time these cards were printed and the fifties?"

"Good question, and don't think I haven't studied on it some. The way I see it, every legend or myth must grow out of some germ of truth. You just gotta know where to separate the wheat from the chaff. Don't you ever get the feeling there's a presence at Christmas time? People talk about the Christmas spirit, but maybe it's more than a *mood.* Maybe it's like in that Dickens story, where there's a *ghost* of Christmas. And maybe there's a bad spirit, as well as the good. You can't have one without the other."

Lefty shrugged. "I guess so."

"Sure. And they stopped printing the cards and things with Krampus on them. If people didn't think about him, seems to me that would drain his power down a mite? So he slinks off somewhere to hide. And where does he go?"

"To Carbon Hill," Lefty ventured a guess.

"Exactly!" Strecker grinned again. "Maybe you're not so stupid after all. This place is known as the town that was built on coal. The mine tunnels go way into the hills. Perfect place for the likes of Krampus to hole up and wait for folks to start believing again. And maybe before the coal ran dry, the miners tunneled a bit too deep."

"And just maybe they woke up your Christmas Bane?"

"Give the boy a gold star, yes! It coulda happened that way. Why not?" Then Strecker unsnapped his breast pocket and brought out a cellophane-wrapped cheese Danish. "Figured I'd do my Christianly duty, tell you the score and bring you this. Something to offer to the Christmas Bane tonight. You unwrap this and stick it outside your cell before you hit the sack and you should be fine."

Lefty shook his head. "You're serious. You really believe this crap?"

"Look, Bohach, it doesn't matter what I believe. Yeah, there have been a lot of people who've seen this jake at one time or another. Upright citizens I have no reason to doubt. But it's up to you to weigh what I told you and decide for yourself."

Lefty shook his head. "Sounds like a buncha townies scarin' one another. What do they call it. . . mass hysteria?"

Strecker's eyes narrowed to slits. "Could be, but are you willing to take that chance?" He shoved the Danish through, but since Lefty didn't reach for it, it fell to the cell floor. "Do what you like. Leastways I'll be able to sleep now that I done my good deed."

With exaggerated purpose, Lefty picked up the pastry, walked to the wastebasket, and dropped it in.

"Suit yourself," Strecker said. He checked his watch. "Ten-thirty-five. Guess that gives you just shy of an hour and a half to repent or leave out some food. But I don't reckon you'll do either. Headin' out now. The sergeant'll look in on you from time to time. Been nice knowin' you, Bohach."

He gave Lefty a final cigarette and one match to light it—one last smoke for the condemned man.

The fire door slammed shut and the overhead lights winked out.

*   *   *

In the darkness of his cell, Lefty listened to the wind howl outside. The furnace vents weren't kicking out heat like they should, so he pulled the second blanket up to his chin. And he mulled over all that Strecker had told him about Carbon Hill's seasonal bogeyman.

Crazy stuff, sure, but he couldn't help thinking it wouldn't hurt to leave out a little food and honor the local tradition. It wouldn't mean he bought into it or anything like that. It would be more like knocking on wood or sidestepping a ladder. When in Hicksville, why not do as the hicks?

In spite of his previous brave front, Lefty felt around in the darkness, then took the Danish out of the wastebasket. He also fumbled around for the greasy paper plate he'd eaten his dinner off of. He popped open the cellophane of the pastry, laid it on the paper plate, and arranged everything beyond the cell bars. Then he licked the icing from his fingers and lay back on the cot.

It was only through the thin beginnings of sleep that he later heard the courthouse clock strike eleven.

*   *   *

"Whazzat?"

Lefty awakened with the sensation that someone was close by. It was as though the someone was staring at him.

He would have shrugged it off if not for the thick, nasally breathing coming from beyond the cell bars. The fog of sleep lifted as Lefty thought, *It's that desk sergeant come for a bed check. That's all.*

But no flashlight swept over his cell, and after a moment or two, there came a clicking sound.

As of hooves clomping on the linoleum.

The Christmas Bane? Lefty thought. *No friggin' way. . .*

And yet whoever was standing beyond the cell door squatted, groping at the Danish. Lefty's pulse elevated slightly at the idea of what might be in the darkness with only a few metal bars separating them.

Then came the sound of the Danish being slurped down.

Lefty drew away from the bars. He could almost sense the stranger's head swiveling at the rustle of blankets.

But he knew there was no such thing as the Christmas Bane. No how. No way. Had to be that Strecker's idea of a joke. Get the prisoner riled with some outlandish tale then scare the cheese out of him later. Well, Lefty Bohach wasn't a guy to be played. He searched his pocket for the match Strecker had left him. It didn't light right off. Not on the first or second try. But on the third, the flame threw a small glow within the cell.

And beyond the rungs was a face, which looked as though it hadn't seen the light of day for years. It also had curving horns and a head-full of picket teeth.

Its mouth split into a grin when its feral saucer eyes locked onto Lefty's.

"Ah! Someone left Krampus a Christmas goose." The words came in a thick, phlegmy wheeze. *"How thoughtful!"*

And as the devil-thing's body pressed impossibly through the cell bars like putty and reform on the other side, Lefty realized he'd been had. The Danish hadn't been to *appease* the Christmas Bane; it had been the bait to draw him in all along. An appetizer to the main course of Lefty's own soul.

*   *   *

Chief Dalton Strecker leaned against the fire door listening. The screams had stopped, and now came a sound like an ear of corn being shucked as Lefty Bohach's spirit was stripped from his body.

At first light, they'd take Lefty's car to the junkyard and reduce it to a solid block of scrap metal. Strecker shoved the Bohach file into the office shredder, erasing the only other shred of proof he'd ever been here. Bohach hadn't even been able to call a lawyer yet because of the holiday. If Carbon Hill could be so lucky every year, Strecker pondered, they'd never lose another citizen.

The Courthouse clock rounded out twelve o'clock. It was officially Christmas, and Krampus would soon rest another year.

48

6
Smoke In A Bottle

By Steve Rasnic Tem

Daddy had the five beer bottles, their labels peeled off, lined up on the shelf. Then he puffed and puffed on his cigarette, packing the smoke into his mouth, making his eyes go funny because that was part of the show. Moving fast he put his mouth over each bottle, filled it with smoke, capped it with an old bottle cap, moved to the next. When he was done he had five bottles full of smoke.

He held each one in front of the fire, turning it so that the smoke flowed, curled inside, made patterns, made faces, weird shapes dancing. Then he'd flip off the cap and the smoke escaped as fast as anything, leaving behind a little stink, that was all.

"Smoke in a bottle, kids," he'd say. "That's all it is. Just like people."

Then he'd sway like a ruined house in a hurricane wind, and sometimes he'd stagger around the room. We knew Christmas was over when Dad fell into the Christmas tree.

So maybe Dad didn't fall into the Christmas tree *every* year. Maybe it was only seven or eight years out of ten. But fall he did, and although it made our mother every way of being angry and frustrated, it made us kids laugh every time, even when he broke something. He was a man of simple entertainments, using the things he always had with him—cigarettes and beer bottles mostly, and a damaged sense of balance—but his act always worked with us.

I hadn't been back in St. Charles in twenty years. Not because I hated it. When you live in a place as poor as that people think you must hate it and you can't wait to leave. I knew I was poor but I didn't know I was *that* poor. I got fed and I lived in the prettiest, greenest place I've ever known—southwest Virginia. Did you know the early Indians called Lee County "Paradise"?

As my cheap rental car rounded the bend I thought the town was on fire. Gray clouds drifted along the road, piled up in front of the car, broke apart and ran away. I rolled my window down and realized it was just morning mist, but there was this sharp scent that burned the nose, like cigarette smoke.

I drove slowly into town. The road had been patched so much it looked like an asphalt quilt. I'd kept a picture of the town in my memory but from the looks of things big chunks were missing, buildings cut out, blown away, replaced by weeds, worn out trailers, and a few hollow stores leaning like dozing drunks. No signs of Christmas, no lights, no street decorations.

In the forties and fifties St. Charles had thousands of people, with restaurants and stores and even a small movie theater. The valley's narrow there, so they built everything down close to the highway. A concrete sidewalk on each side didn't leave much room for road. On Saturday nights the road shrank down to one lane and you could barely get through. You could hear the party all through the valley, or so Daddy used to tell us. By my time in the late sixties St. Charles was falling asleep.

Daddy drank a lot and worked only occasionally. These days you'd call him an alcoholic. I didn't know that word when I was a kid.

I knew there was still a lot good about the town, but it's not the kind of place you come back to. No jobs to speak of since the mines shut down. And part of getting older is looking back and understanding how much you didn't have.

The first Christmas I remember from elementary school we had to draw names and get a present for one of our classmates. The night before the party our mother sat the three of us down and handed us each a pack of chewing gum and helped us wrap them up fancy in a cloth package with dress ribbon and a quilting square. She showed us how to hold the scissors and where to cut the cloth and how to split and fold the ribbon until at the end we had three unique flowers attached to these beautiful little packages.

Because the girl I gave the gum to had been brought up right, she made herself smile when she thanked me politely. But I knew exactly what disappointment looked like. At the end of the day I saw her talking to her mom and showing the gum. Her mom looked at me then, not in a mean way but like she was measuring me for a suit. That was the first time I ever felt really poor.

Dad died from lung disease shortly after my freshman year in college and I went home for his funeral, then I came back again for my sister's wedding. And this last time for my mother's funeral while I was going through a divorce. That good woman never even met my kids. Three times in all those years. I'm not proud of that.

The house had been sold to an investor. When my brother and sister asked me if I could clean it out, I agreed, even though that was the last thing I wanted to do for Christmas. It was the least I could do. I wasn't going to see my kids until after the holiday anyway. You could say a lot bad about my dad, but at least he was there every Christmas.

Our old house had lost most of its yard and the sheltering trees, and a tangle of weeds and rusted metal hugged the foundation. I parked where my mother's flowerbeds used to be. Inside, the light was yellow from weak lamps and sun burning through brittle shades, furry dust over everything, as if some of that amber light had disintegrated into a thick layer of brown. I felt like holding my breath—it was like trying to breathe inside a grave. I wondered if this was anything like what my dad experienced all those years ago while his lungs were failing.

In one room I counted six cheap headboards, nine sets of bedsprings, a box full of wheels, two rotting pillows jammed into the corner, a dark, viscous stain on the top one. All would go in the trash.

The smallest bedroom was empty, except for some mud and grease on the floor. This had been Ann's. She was the youngest and always had the smallest room. My bedroom was a long, narrow room along the back of the house, like a closet. It still had a tiny little bookcase. I couldn't really find myself in that room, but I did remember that bookcase. It had never held more than a few books. One Christmas my mother had given me two—*The Adventures of Robin Hood* and *The Legends of King Arthur*. She couldn't have paid much, but she'd been so happy to give them to me. I'd read them over and over until they fell apart.

My brother's room was just an empty box. Mom and Daddy's room was on the other side of the house. This was where my mother died. It still had her bed, her dresser, her night table, and a picture of an Indian in a canoe on the wall. It still looked like a real room, like she'd just stepped out to pick flowers for the dinner table.

I smelled cigarette smoke. I looked around and saw the brown silhouette on the shade, the figure outside swaying, probably drunk, struggling to hold onto his cigarette. By the time I got outside he was gone.

I looked across the yard at my neighbor's house: a man standing on the porch, smoking.

"Can I help you?" I could hear my voice shaking.

"Don't need no help."

"Were you just in my yard?"

"Nosir. Is that *your* yard?"

"My mother lived here."

"Hey! Hey, Willie? Is that you?"

I grabbed some chairs, and my old friend Eddie and I sat in the empty living room, mostly just staring at each other. We'd both changed a lot, Eddie more visibly. He weighed about half what he once had, and he had tattoos, and about half a goatee, as if something had eaten the right side of it. Eddie finally broke the silence with "So, you got any beers?"

I carried the six-pack in from the car. I gave him the whole thing.

"You're not drinking?"

"Not tonight," I said. Actually I almost never drink. I had no idea why I'd bought the beer. "Just give me the empties."

He stared at the bottles dubiously. "What? They collectible?"

"No. I just thought I'd put them on that shelf over the fireplace, like Dad used to."

He squinted at the thin piece of wood. "I remember that. Hope they don't fall off—looks a little crooked." He started on the first one, then stopped, raising it in my direction. "Merry Christmas." He drank a few swallows, then said, "Your dad fell into the Christmas tree one year, didn't he?"

"Six or seven years, actually."

"Yeah. I remember laughing about it. There were some years I wish my family had had something like that to laugh about. But six or seven times? Even if you're drinking heavy, that's kind of, unusual."

We didn't talk much after that—just the occasional burst of words, with long periods of silence in between. I didn't mind—that was what a conversation was in St. Charles. He'd tell me something about his life now, and he'd tell me about some classmate or other, who had died, divorced, or disappeared from that part of the country, never to be seen again. Periodically he'd hand me an empty beer bottle and I'd scrape the label off and balance it on the shelf.

As the night wore on I moved the old lamps from my mother's room in for more light, but the best I could accomplish was a few bright patches of brilliance and a great deal of dirty shadow that seemed to float along the walls and over the ceiling, making the house appear to sway, as if I were the one drinking. Eddie, on the other hand, seemed like the sober one, talking more as the hours passed of people and events I'd largely forgotten.

"You remember Jack Gilford, don't you?"

"Sure. Is he dead, too?"

"No, but he oughta be," Eddie said, giggling. "A mite cold in here, don't you think? Why don't you start something in that fireplace?"

I was surprised to find about an inch of snow on the ground. *You got snow, you're a rich man*, was something Daddy used to say. I'd understood that even as a kid. Snow was good for covering up shabbiness, and ugliness, and essentials missing. It even had a way of transforming those things into something quaint, suitable for a picture postcard.

I looked across the valley at the pinpricks of light floating down like slow-falling stars, and the steam from chimneys floating up, columns like vague figures standing on rooftops, watching. I couldn't see the main road from our old house, but I could hear the busy traffic and all those people.

I stopped moving. What was I thinking? Those noises were from another time, and I couldn't be hearing them now. It had to be some distortion in the air that had caused the effect, some echo off the stripped-to-rock hills. I heard coughing, a drawn-out wheeze. I went to the edge of the window and peeked inside. Eddie was peacefully drinking, head tilted back and lips around the bottle's mouth. And I heard the wheeze again, followed by the bone-rattling cough. I looked around. A few yards away a man stood with his back to me, wearing

54

nothing out there in the cold but a T-shirt and boxer shorts. He coughed again, his whole body shaking, hunched shoulders seeming to broaden, as if in advance of some transformation. I ran a couple of feet to the wall and grabbed some wood stacked there, ran inside without looking back. I bumped against the wall in my haste and one of the beer bottles tumbled to the floor into an explosion of glass. "Sorry," I said.

"No biggie, bro. I'll have a replacement for you in just a sec."

I said nothing to Eddie about what I had seen and heard. I built a fire—it was a little smoky, there was probably debris blocking part of the chimney. But we tolerated it, even though it made us cry a little. After Eddie left there were scattered voices in the smoke, but I learned to tolerate them as well.

Early next morning Eddie showed up with a serious face, dragging a small white pine nailed to a crude base of crossed scrap wood. "Christmas Eve, Willie. I reckon you need a tree." He grinned then, and in the burning glare off the snow I saw that he had numerous missing teeth. "Don't worry—I didn't steal it. It was in my back yard."

Eddie left to spend the next several days with family in Tennessee. I dragged the tree in and put it in the corner of the living room, sat down in a chair and spent some time staring at it. It leaned quite a bit, but still managed to stay up. I decided then to find something to put on it—I knew I'd feel even worse about the day if I left it bare.

I hadn't been down in the cellar since we found that rat the size of a beaver when I was nine years old. The rats used to scrabble out of the abandoned mines and sneak into town. About the only way to get rid of them was a shotgun. But that's where my mother always kept the tree decorations, and anything else she didn't want us kids to mess with.

The light fixture still worked, but it was like a candle at the opening of a mine. Inside it smelled like rotting vegetables and spoiled meat. The invisible walls were lined with mason jars whose dark contents absorbed just enough light to make me avoid them. I found the damp cardboard box with the decorations halfway in, pulling it close even as something scurried out of it. To my credit I didn't drop the box, but hurried upstairs and shoved it by the tree.

After a couple of years of Dad wiping out the Christmas tree, my mother had put her favorite decorations on the shelf by the beer bottles rather than risk them. There the glass angel and the ceramic deer and the little Santa Claus had had a perfect view of Dad's mysterious smoking bottles. I didn't need to be so cautious, and nestled them right into the front branches where I could see them. None of the colored lights lit reliably so I didn't bother with them. But I did discover that lighting a fire in the fireplace created interesting reflections in the shiny colored balls and fragments of icicle I scraped out of the bottom of the box. Shards of rainbow swam in the walls as an untraceable draft lightly stirred the branches. I wished my kids could see it.

I wasn't even sure what we'd gotten the kids for Christmas that year. Since they were all going to be at her parents' house she'd handled everything, and I hadn't even asked.

This tree had no presents under it, but there had never been many presents under the tree in this house.

I must have dozed off, and when I woke up I was sure I'd caught the house on fire—I smelled burning—wood and plastic, paper and cloth, a world of things turned to smoke and drifting into my nose and mouth. I gaped at the fireplace, my eyes blurry.

On the shelf smoke boiled in and out of the remaining bottles. I walked over for a better view: although smoke carved the air in all five, in the two on the end it swirled into miniature, fiery galaxies before floating up the necks and out into the room where they joined the shadows flowing across the ceiling.

I could hear a soft wheeze behind me but I could not bring myself to turn around. Instead I walked into my mother's old bedroom and went to sleep on her oval rug.

I found the Christmas tree lying on the floor the next morning, a great dent on the ceiling-facing side, branches pushed aside and broken as if from a great weight.

It's funny how sometimes you have all the evidence right in front of you, but yet it takes you years to give it the proper importance. A man doesn't accidentally fall into a Christmas tree seven out of ten years even if he is a drunk. And his wife doesn't just put up with that kind of behavior. It had all been an act for the benefit of my brother, my sister, and me. I remembered how in those years when we kids got practically nothing on Christmas morning Dad always told his best stories and did his best tricks to entertain us, to distract us. And we couldn't help but laugh when he swayed and stumbled and fell into that poor, blameless tree.

There on the shelf were the glass angel and the ceramic deer and the little Santa Claus, safe as houses.

Christmas was over. I spent the day cleaning and throwing the remaining pieces of that old life away (save three ornaments). The next day I would drive to the coast and see my kids.

7

The Nativity Tray

By Sara J. Larson

The dashboard clock read 2:00 p.m. on Christmas Eve as I drove up the steep gravel driveway of the time-share cabin at the Cumberland Plateau Resort. I set my parking brake and pondered chocking the wheels with chunks of the gray stone retaining wall, but I was too tired.

This Appalachian terrain weirded me out. I lived in a horizontal landscape, and the relentless verticals of Tennessee crowded me with claustrophobic vertigo. Everything went straight up. Even the mountains came to a point, not like the soft, rounded hills I knew. I opened the trunk and pulled out a plastic bag of groceries, a small suitcase, and a brown paper shopping bag. The shopping bag held a tiny prelit Christmas tree, an impulse buy at the Cracker Barrel where I ordered, but didn't eat, lunch. Bags in hand, I trudged up the walk and unlocked the cabin door.

I was in Tennessee because I couldn't bear to be home. Home meant Indiana, Indianapolis specifically, my house in particular. Home, with the blue slate flagstone walk that led to the flower-edged driveway. The walk where I stood on a September morning, waving goodbye to Dan, and to eight-year-old Gabriella, safely belted into the backseat of our SUV. I waved as they pulled out of the driveway. Watched as Dan drove into the path of a city garbage truck that hit them broadside and made me a widow and the mother of a dead child.

The resort directory listed the occupancy of the cabin at two. They exaggerated. Downstairs consisted of a kitchenette at one end, a loveseat and chair in front of a shoebox-sized fireplace at the other. "Mass produced rustic" best described the decor. Pressed wood shaped into tree trunks formed the legs of the tables and the upholstered furniture. Said upholstery sported a pine-needle-and-cone motif in maroon and hunter green. Bad wildlife prints festooned the walls. Gabby would have loved it. Dan would have fallen down laughing. I didn't care enough to have an opinion. The tiny staircase against the back wall climbed to the bedroom at such a steep angle it was practically a ladder. I scaled it to find more prints of bears and deer, and a bed decked in a comforter and shams with blue and white silhouettes of wolves.

I unpacked my suitcase; what little I brought fit in one dresser drawer. At the bottom of the suitcase lay a box tied with string. My tears blistered the shiny white cardboard lid as I carried it downstairs and collapsed into the chair.

I don't know how long I sat, watching my brain replay those few seconds when a trash truck changed everything. When I looked up, dusk had fallen. My groceries sat on the tiny kitchen table, my TV dinners thawing. As I put them in the freezer, I saw the empty ice cube trays. I'd just have to drink my Coke warm tonight.

Carrying the glass back to the chair, I picked up the box and contemplated the knotted string.

Before my world turned hollow, Gabby and I had a special Christmas Eve ritual. The Nativity Tray. According to medieval legend, if a person braves the cold on Christmas Eve with a tray bearing a bone for a stray dog, some hay for a weary horse, clothing for a cold traveler, a garland for one who has been shackled, food for the songbirds, and sugarplums for poor children, that person will receive all the gifts Heaven has to bestow. Memories unspooled of Gabby kneeling beside me on the cold ground, arranging Milk Bones and pieces of fudge on our tray. One year, she saw a huge, fourteen dollar smoked bone in the grocery store pet section and came close to throwing a tantrum to get me to buy it. Now I wished I had.

One tug undid the knot, revealing my pathetic offerings to Heaven. A single Milk Bone, dry lawn clippings, six inches of plastic ivy, a handful of bird-seed, and peppermints cadged from a restaurant bowl. I rummaged in the kitchen cabinets until I found a cookie sheet, and carried it out to the car. The wind bit me, and I regretted not at least grabbing gloves. I pulled a beat up jacket out of the trunk, a fake-sheepskin lined corduroy horror of Dan's. He loved that coat, and finally, it got so ratty I refused to be seen with him in it. "Why do you want to go around looking like a homeless person?" I asked him. He kept it in the SUV, in a box with the jumper cables, "in case of emergency". I knew he wore it when I wasn't around. Now I held it up to my face, trying to catch his scent.

I slammed the trunk lid and walked to the edge of the tree line. The pines climbed straight up the side of the mountain, trapping me in the bottom of a dark pit. I knelt to lay the tray on the brown, crunchy grass, and the coat beside it. I stared at the pitiful scraps on the cheap aluminum tray. Who was I kidding? What I needed I would never have again, no matter what bribe I tendered. Tears rose again, stinging my eyes. I bent forward until my forehead touched the ground, the sobs choking me. I cried until I ran out of tears, then heaved myself up. A voice spoke.

"Ma'am, can I have that?"

On the opposite side of my tray was a boy. He looked about twelve, right in the middle of the all-elbows-and-kneecaps stage. Bony wrists stuck out below the cuffs of his flannel shirt, and the hem of his jeans didn't quite make it to the tops of his worn shoes. He had no coat, gloves, or hat; his black hair ruffled in the wind, and his lips were blue with cold.

"Wha-what?" I asked.

"Can I have that coat, ma'am?" He pointed at Dan's jacket. "It's mighty cold."

"Of course you can. Here." I shook the pine needles off, and held it out.

"Much obliged, ma'am." As he slipped his arms into the sleeves, his eyes flashed up toward mine. Brown, shy, but warm. He shrugged to settle the coat and shoved his hands into the pockets. His expression changed to consternation as he held out the old gloves he found tucked in them.

"You can have those, too." Another quick look, this time with a fleeting smile. He started to walk away.

"What are you doing out here, anyway?" I asked. He stopped, shrugged, and stared at the ground.

"Why don't you come in for a little while? I was just getting ready to fix supper. You could get warm."

"Oh, no, ma'am, I don't want to put you out none." This time he looked me full in the face and I could see the freckles sprinkled across his nose.

"You're not putting me out. I don't have much, just TV dinners and canned soup, but you're welcome. Let's get you warmed up and fed, then I'll drive you home." I put my arm around his shoulders and led him into the cabin.

I bustled around, building a fire, getting out bowls and spoons, folding the paper towels to look more like napkins. The boy, wrapped in Dan's coat, sat staring into the fire.

"What's your name?" I asked, emptying the soup into a pan.

"Leroy. Most people call me Lee."

"I'm Shelly Caldwell. Does your family live around here?"

"I live with my brother, he works in the mine. My folks have passed." His face looked weary and resigned, like an old man's. Then he smiled and the just-past-little-boy came flooding back. "Somethin' smells good!"

"I thought a grilled cheese sandwich would go with the soup. It was my daughter's favorite." The pain flashed through me. Shoving it down, I kept talking. "So, I'll drive you to your brother's after we eat, okay?" I poured the soup into bowls and set the sandwich plates on the table.

He ate like food had just been invented. Before he was finished, I'd opened another can of soup, brought out the saltines, and toasted two more cheese sandwiches. Not wanting to interrupt his enjoyment, I ate in silence. When he mopped up the last of his soup with the crust of his final sandwich, and drained his fourth glass of milk, I broached the question again.

"We should think about getting you home," I said, loading the dishes into the tiny dishwasher.

"I don't want to put you out none, Miz Caldwell. You been so nice." He stood, buttoning the jacket.

"Call me Shelly."

"Okay Miz Shelly. But I don't want to be no trouble."

"No, I insist," I replied. "It's nearly eleven o'clock and freezing cold. Just tell me how to get to your brother's; it can't be far."

The boy blushed, shook his head, opened his mouth, shut it.

"Leroy." He shifted from one foot to the other.

"Lee, look at me." His brown eyes inched up to meet mine. They were wide and glinted with tears.

"I can't get in the house."

"What?"

"My brother's wife, she don't like me, don't want me there. When Melvin took me in after our folks died, she said I could only come in to sleep. If I'm not there when she thinks I oughta be, she locks me out." His face was red and tears clung to his lashes.

"But that's ridiculous! She locked you out *tonight*? That's why you were wandering in the woods without a coat?"

He nodded.

"Well, we'll see about that." I went to the closet and pulled spare bedding from the shelf. "I'll make up the couch for you to sleep on, and tomorrow we'll see what the sheriff has to say."

Closing the closet door, I caught a glimpse of the Cracker Barrel sack in the corner. The gold plastic star on the tree caught the light.

"We've even got a tree," I said, placing it on the end table. "Now, you get comfy on that sofa, and I'll go make cocoa. You're a little too old for Santa Claus." He grinned up at me. "But we have the tree and the fire, and in the morning, I'll make you some toaster waffles. How's that sound?"

His shoes and coat stacked in a neat pile by the door, he curled onto the loveseat and pulled the blanket close. I made the cocoa mix with milk, the way Gabby liked it. Like every kid, she preferred the mix, with its gritty dehydrated marshmallows, to homemade. As I stirred it, the smell released memories of Gabby perched on a chair, chattering about her school day. I scrubbed the tears away with a potholder and poured the cocoa. When I handed him the cup, Lee wrapped both hands around its warmth. Closing his eyes, he lowered his face to the fragrant steam, inhaling luxuriously before he drank.

I turned out the lights. The little tree and the fireplace glowed. I found a Christmas program on TV, a PBS station airing some pops concert. I sipped my hot chocolate, stared into the flames, and lost myself in the music.

It was the silence that brought me back. The station had signed off for the night, nothing on the screen but the PBS logo. I looked at the sleeping boy. I bent over to tuck him in, and my hand brushed the black hair, soft as kitten fur, soft as Gabby's, off his forehead.

"Goodnight, Lee," I whispered, kissing the crown of his head. He sighed and snuggled deeper into his pillow. I dragged myself up the stairs to the bedroom.

I woke disoriented by the strange bed. The quiet of the mountains left me feeling like I wanted to pop my ears. Then I remembered the boy downstairs.

There was nothing on the sofa but a pillow hollowed in the shape of a boy's head.

Three minutes later I pulled into the lot at the tiny convenience store nestled at the base of the main resort drive.

"Merry Christmas!" the woman behind the counter called out over the jingle bells on the door. "Glad you stopped in this morning. We're closing at noon for the holiday."

I leaned on the counter, catching my breath. "Can you tell me how to get in touch with Child Protective Services?"

"That's the sheriff." She pulled out a cell phone. "What's goin' on?"

"There was a boy up by my cabin last night, who said his sister-in-law locked him out of the house. His name was Leroy."

Glass shattered in one of the aisles and the spicy tang of sweet pickles filled the air. A man stepped out, his pants splashed with pickle juice, his right hand hanging like it still held the jar. "Oh, my God, she's seen Shivering Lee," he said.

I turned to the woman. She, too, stood frozen, cell phone halfway to her ear.

I looked from one to the other. "Shivering Lee?"

"Tell her the story, Crystal," the pickle man said.

"It's a local legend."

"Legend, my foot," he said.

"Do you want to tell it, Jimmy?" Crystal glared at him.

"My bad. Go ahead. It gives me the creeps."

"Anyway," she resumed. "The *story* says there was this boy named Leroy, but everybody called him Lee. His parents died and his brother had to take him in, and the brother's wife didn't like him. So she made him stay outside all day. When he wasn't in school, he rode his bike all over town, just to have something to do. And whenever she got the chance she would lock him outside for the night."

"He didn't have a bike," I said, groping for a rational rebuttal. "When was this supposed to have happened?"

"During the Depression," Jimmy said. "Lotta folks were having a hard time. The mine was played out and down more than it was open. Nobody wanted an extra mouth to feed."

"He said his brother worked in the mine." I couldn't get my mind around this.

"The mine closed for good in '53," Crystal put in.

"What happened to him?" I said, not wanting to know.

"One night she locked him out, came a cold snap, and he froze to death," Crystal said. "They say he goes around, scratching on folk's windows, wanting to come inside and get warm. People look out and see him shivering with blue lips and his eyelashes covered with frost."

"That's how they found him, all blue and stuff." Jimmy shuddered. "Oh, that gives me the willies."

"He slept on my sofa," I whispered, feeling like ice water ran down my back. "I cooked him soup."

"Lady, you just spent the night with a ghost."

"Jimmy, will you take your pickles and get outta here before Janice comes lookin'? I'll clean up the mess." We watched Jimmy get into his F-150. Crystal shook her head. "Jimmy's a nut for ghost stories. He gets all worked up every time he sees a shadow."

"This time he may have been right." I left her standing there with her mouth hanging open, still holding her cell phone.

*　　*　　*

A small, sturdy figure wearing a corduroy jacket and gloves stood out behind the cabin in front of the pine trees.

"Lee?" I called. He waved. I crossed the clearing and seized his shoulders.

"I just wanted to say thanks, Miz Shelly, for lettin' me get warm." His red lips parted in a smile. "I feel so much better. Do you feel better, Miz Shelly?"

I hugged his warm, solid little body. Did I feel better? I examined the Dan-and-Gabby shaped hole in my soul. The pain lingered, but it wasn't raw. Not healed, not yet, but at least scabbed over.

"Yes, I feel better." I kissed the top of his head. "Thank you."

"I'm glad. We helped each other. I have to go now. Bye, Miz Shelly." His arms tightened around my waist in a final hug.

"Why can't you stay?" I asked.

"Nobody can stay, not like they want to."

And I let him go. I let them all go. He didn't pop out of existence like a conjurer's rabbit. He just faded away until nothing remained but the warmth against my body. A breeze stirred the pine needles where he'd stood.

"You're welcome, Lee," I whispered. I looked down at the cookie sheet at my feet.

The Nativity Tray was empty.

8

Apple Head Dolly

By Scott Nicholson

An orange.

A freakin' orange.

Willard rummaged in the stocking one more time, just to be sure. Times were tough all over, especially in the disconnected little corner of the world known as Windshake, North Carolina, and even the mountain folk who prided themselves on independence still had to drive to Wal-mart for their toilet paper and the Goodson Paper Mill for their paychecks. The recession was something the old-timers complained about around the general-store wood stove, but it was mostly something wrote up in the newspapers, and Willard had never been much of a hand at reading.

Still, an orange? Nothing else?

"Something the matter, Willard?" Daddy asked.

"Not really."

Daddy was sharpening the chainsaw blade, running the file between the grooves. Daddy had a tough time of it, because one arm ended in a nub between his elbow and his wrist.

Momma griped when he did mechanic work on the kitchen table, but as Daddy liked to say, if you couldn't fix it yourself, you ought not eat it. Willard never figured out what that meant but Daddy said it like there was no room for argument.

Grampap was asleep in the ragged recliner, his head tilted back and his mouth open. His teeth were in the jar beside him, and a strand of drool trailed down onto his filthy longhandles. He snored, and the noise fell in rhythm with the rasping of Daddy's file. Now Willard understood why they called it "sawing wood."

"I got a dolly," Sue Beth said. Sue Beth was seven, so it was only fair that she got the better presents, because she still believed in Santa Claus and the folks had to put on a show. Willard was 10 and figured this was probably the last year he got any toys at all. Come next Christmas, he'd be getting hand tools.

Sue Beth held up her doll. It had a shriveled apple for a head. The way Momma told it, you cut little holes for the mouth and eyes, then when the apple shriveled up and dried, you had a face. Momma had tied some brown yarn to the stem for hair, then stitched together a few rags to make a dress.

"What you gonna name it?" Daddy asked Sue Beth.

"Dolly," she said. Sue Beth had never had much imagination, which Willard figured was just as well. All imagination had ever done for him was cause him misery. He imagined all the in-town boys with their new sleds, their shotguns, their video games, and their big, fat stockings full of candy.

"That's a nice name," Momma said, wiping her hands on her apron. She was cooking up the Christmas dinner, a tough old tom turkey that should have been killed three or four holidays back. Potatoes, cornbread, and some canned green beans would round out the meal, and there was a blackberry cobbler in the oven that made the house smell good, even over the sweaty stink of Grampap's flannel underwear.

Willard couldn't help but notice Sue Beth's bulging stocking. It hung from the clothesline, since they didn't have a fireplace mantel. The clothesline stretched across the living room, and you had to duck under it to get to the little bedrooms in the back of the house. Willard shared a room with his sister, and that was getting kind of awkward, because he didn't have any pajamas that fit.

"What else did Santa bring you?" Daddy asked, but he said it like he wasn't listening.

"Willard got a ball," she said.

"Ain't no ball." He tossed the orange in the air and caught it.

"How come I don't got no orange ball?"

"It ain't a ball, it's an orange," he said.

"Like an apple, except it's orange," Momma said.

Sue Beth should have known what an orange was, even if they hardly ever bought them in the grocery store. That's how they taught you the color in elementary school. They showed you a picture of an orange and then the teacher said the word "orange." But like all the other dirty tricks of school, you couldn't count on it, because the very next minute, they'd show you a picture of a lemon and say "yellow" instead of "lemon." Daddy said that was just the way of the world and that's why you should never trust books.

"How come I don't get no orange?" Sue Beth asked with a whine in her voice.

"Because they're 'spensive," Momma said. "They come all the way from other countries, like Florida and Californey. Besides, you got an apple."

"When we was kids, we'd get one orange for the whole family," Daddy said, resting for a second. "We'd slice it up eight ways. You kids don't know how tough the times used to be up here in the mountains."

Actually, Willard did know, because Daddy told that story about four times every Christmas, even when they didn't have any oranges in their stockings. Daddy would go on about how Grampap used to carve toys for all the kids, and from the looks of the old man's cracked and scarred hands, Willard believed him. But somehow Grampap had managed to keep all his fingers and both his hands, unlike Daddy.

"Why don't you look in your stocking, Sue Beth?" Momma said.

Sue Beth grinned and hugged Dolly to her chest. The clothesline was a little above her reach, so she grabbed the toe of the old sock and yanked. It flopped loose and an avalanche of peppermints and butterscotch came tumbling to the linoleum. Sue Beth squealed in delight. Willard watched one of the peppermints roll under Grampap's chair.

"Now look at this mess," Momma said. "Help her, Willard."

Sue Beth knelt on the floor and gathered the candy. Besides the hard pieces wrapped in plastic, there were a few bits of foil that looked like chocolate. One of them had a picture of a reindeer on it. While Willard scraped the candy into a big pile, Sue Beth peeled a piece open. It was a chocolate Santa. She bit its head off.

As Willard shoved her candy back into the stocking, he kept an eye on the piece that had disappeared under Grampap's chair. When the sock was full, Willard passed it to his sister. It was so heavy she could barely lift it.

"Time for dinner," Momma said. "Willard, will you wake up Grampap?"

"Reckon I better move the chainsaw," Daddy said.

"Just don't start it in here," she replied. "Last time, we about choked to death on the fumes."

"If you can't fix it, you ought not eat it," he said.

"Well, just get it out of here so I can set the table."

While Daddy took the chainsaw to the shed, leaving the front door open long enough for some snow to blow in, Willard shook Grampap's elbow. Grampap stopped snoring but didn't move. His face was blank and he looked dead, but nothing unusual about that. Momma was busy at the stove, so Willard knelt down and reached under the chair. He raked through the dust and wadded-up paper and cigarette butts until he felt the piece of candy, then he squirreled it away in his pocket.

He gave Grampap's shoulder a shove, and the old man jerked forward as if he were on wires, blinking and wheezing. "Whu–where—shot who?"

"Time for Christmas dinner, Grampap," Willard said.

"Christmas?" He rubbed his cheek as if it belonged to someone else's face and he wasn't used to the wrinkles. "I didn't even know it was winter yet."

"It happened sometime after Thanksgiving," Momma said.

"I got a dolly," Sue Beth said, holding the apple-head doll out to Grampap.

Grampap squinted at it with his milky eyes. "Apple head, huh? Whose hair it got on it?"

"It's yarn," Momma said.

"Well, that's good." He put in his teeth and his words were clearer now. "You don't need to be messing around with no poppets."

"It's not no puppet, it's a doll," Sue Beth said. She was used to Grampap not being able to hear too good.

"A 'poppet' is what they call it when it's got somebody's hair on it," Momma said. "In the old days, folks believed you could hurt people you didn't like if you made a poppet out of them."

"It wasn't just in the old days," Grampap said. "When your daddy was eight, he spelled a neighbor who stole his fishing pole. Clancy Wheeler was his name, part of them Wheelers on the back side of Elk Knob."

"Clancy the school bus driver that only got three fingers?" Willard said. He wondered why Clancy always looked at them funny when he picked them up in the mornings. Every time Willard stepped on board, it seemed like Clancy was flexing his mangled hand as if wanting to make a claw and strangle him.

"Hush up, Grampap," Momma said. "Don't scare the kids on Christmas."

"Best to know about the ways of the world," Grampap said. "That way, there ain't no surprises."

"Hush up," Momma said, putting the turkey on the table.

They ate until they were full, and Willard had a second piece of cobbler. Daddy had given him a buck knife for Christmas, but he'd tucked it under the Christmas tree so Sue Beth would think it was from Santa Claus. While Sue Beth helped Momma with the dishes, Willard went outside with Daddy to stock the tinderbox. The snow was light but hard, the wind kicking and taking the fun out of it.

"Daddy, what happened to Clancy Wheeler?" Willard asked, rubbing his hands together. The wood was like blocks of ice.

"Nothing that I know of."

"Did you make a poppet out of him?"

"Them old ways is best forgot," Daddy said. "No good ever comes out of them."

"Well, if somebody deserves it, you ought to be able to make them pay for bad things."

"Trouble is, folks ain't so smart when it comes to deciding good and bad."

"If Clancy stole your fishing pole, he done bad."

Daddy knocked the rotted bark off a frozen oak limb. "Grampap's been talking, huh?"

"It come up about poppets."

"Well, Clancy was known to have what we used to call 'sticky fingers.' Couldn't let go of things even if they wasn't his."

"And you made a poppet?"

"I took some hairs out of his baseball cap. He was always one to be losing hairs."

"Fingers, too, by the looks of it."

"When you lay a spell, the punishment fits the crime. He had sticky fingers, all right. Got 'em stuck in a saw blade three weeks later."

"Seems fair to me."

Daddy pushed the nub of his arm against the door. "Maybe so, but poppet spells have a way of coming back on you. Now come on in and forget all that foolishness."

Willard couldn't forget, though. By the time the chores were done, Sue Beth was sitting cross-legged on the floor, yawning and rubbing her eyes. Grampap had already gone to bed. Momma was doing some knitting by the fireplace, taking her turn in the recliner. Daddy settled in with a lawnmower carburetor at the kitchen table. The radio was switched on, piping in some holiday hymns, but it was all organ music and no words so Willard couldn't tell one from another.

"Go on to bed, honey," Momma said to Sue Beth.

"But, Mommy—"

"Don't 'But Mommy' me. Get on."

Sue Beth hugged her dolly to her chest and walked under the clothesline, her stocking trailing behind her on the floor. "Can I take my candy?"

"Sure, but don't put none in your mouth," Momma said. "You're liable to choke."

"I won't."

The house was quiet for a while, Daddy not cussing too much over the stubborn parts and Momma settled in with a shawl she planned to sell at the church bazaar. Willard mostly just stared into the fire, thinking about fingers and apple-head poppets and how sticky butterscotch got after you sucked on it awhile.

"Sure was a good Christmas, wasn't it?" Momma said to Willard.

"Do you like your set of dish towels?" he said. He'd saved up enough to buy four of them at the Dollar General, but only two of them matched.

"That was real sweet," she said.

"When I get big, I'll buy you a whole matching set, plus some place mats to go with it," he said.

"Don't be talking uppity," Daddy said. "Makes it sound like you ain't content with your lot."

"Well, the paper mill said they'd pick back up in the spring," Momma said, with a tired smile. "Things will get better then."

"I ain't counting on that," Daddy said. "Soon as this weather clears, I'll be looking into carpentry work."

Willard didn't say anything. For a few years, rich folks had been building big old mansions on the top of the ridges, but all the best spots were taken and plenty of carpenters were drawing unemployment. Daddy said he wasn't taking no government handouts, and Willard figured that was too bad, because the kids of unemployed carpenters had been getting fancy electronic toys, and all Willard had was an orange and a knife. He kept the orange out of sight, in case Daddy asked him if he'd slice it five ways so everybody could get a taste.

"Well, Merry Christmas, everybody," Momma said, like that was the answer to everything.

"I'm tired," Willard said. "Reckon I'll turn in."

"Don't wake up your sister," Daddy said. "You know how she gets."

"Thanks for the knife," he said. "And the orange."

Willard kept the door cracked so he wouldn't have to turn on the light. Daddy had built a wooden-frame bunk bed for them, and Sue Beth was asleep on the bottom bunk. Willard hid his orange on the shelf, behind a baseball glove and a jar of marbles. Maybe if it dried up, it would make a nice head for a doll, but maybe it only worked with apples. He undressed, feeling the hard knot of candy in his pocket. The air was cold on his naked legs.

"Sue Beth," he whispered.

She snorted a little but didn't answer. The apple-head dolly was tucked beneath her arm, along with the sock full of candy. A couple of wrappers were stuck under her cheek. She'd been eating in bed.

He gripped the stocking and tried to ease it out from under her arm, figuring the chocolate would melt if she slept with it. He was doing her a favor, that was all. He wondered if she'd counted all the pieces. He'd just have a couple, then put the wrappers in bed with her, and she'd figure she must have eaten them while she was falling asleep.

But he'd only slid the sock a few inches before she stirred and tugged the sock to her chest, wrapping her little arm tight around it in a big hug. She must have gotten it mixed up with the dolly, because the dolly rolled away against her pillow, the shriveled apple looking like Grampap in the darkness. Maybe a little family resemblance helped the poppet magic.

He gave the sock one more try, but she stirred and fluttered her eyes. She rolled over until she was mostly on top of it, and he didn't see any way to get to it without waking her up.

He took the knife from his pocket and unfolded it. The blade was sharp. Daddy was handy with a file and a whetstone. It only took a little effort to snip a couple of strands of Sue Beth's hair.

Willard tied them to the apple-head doll. He wondered if you were supposed to say a spell or something. Grampap and Daddy hadn't mentioned it. Let the punishment fit the crime.

He took the piece of candy from his pocket, unwrapped it, and shoved it into the biggest hole in the dried-apple face. He tossed the wrapper onto Sue Beth's pillow, then laid the dolly beside her on the bed.

In the living room, the Christmas hymns were still going. He climbed onto the top bunk, wishing he had some pajamas. The blankets were chilly, but he'd shiver them warm soon enough. Willard fell asleep thinking of all that candy, and how it would soon be his, and how he'd take it to bed with him and sneak pieces into his mouth as he fell asleep.

Something like that, it was bound to give you sweet dreams.

9
Yule Cat

By JG Faherty

Excitement hovered over the town of Fox Run in much the same way the snow-filled clouds had done all week. The day seemed ordinary enough, but children and adults alike knew differently.

Tonight would be special.

All day long, women bustled about in kitchens, grandmothers and mothers and daughters, cooking and baking the feasts for that night. The savory, grease-laden scents of fried ham, roast lamb, and *hamborgarhyryggur*—smoked pork rack—competed with the heavenly aromas of fresh-baked breads and desserts. For those with a sweet tooth, plates stacked high with jelly-covered pancakes and twisted fried dough—*lummer* and *kleinur*—sat on tables and counters, wherever there was room.

It was the traditional Yule feast, part of the celebration of the winter solstice.

The longest night of the year.

The night when ghosts ride the winds and the Yule Cat roams in search of lazy humans to eat.

"Aw, Grandpa, that's just a silly old tale to scare little kids," Jacob Anders said, as his grandfather finished his annual telling of the Yule story.

"Don't talk to your *Farfar* like that," Grandma Anders said, her thin face pulled tight in one of her mock-serious scowls. She worked hard to keep up her brusque appearance to the rest of the family, only occasionally letting her old-country veneer slip, as she'd done earlier when she let Jacob and his older sister Erika lick the spoons after she iced the traditional Yule cake.

Like most of Fox Run's residents, the Anders had emigrated from Scandinavia, eventually settling in Western Pennsylvania, where the Appalachians provided the same backdrop as the *Kölen* of their homeland.

Although they'd celebrated Yule at their grandparents' since before they could remember, this year was the first year Jacob and Erika's parents weren't with them. They'd dropped the children off the day before, with kisses and hugs and promises to return in four days loaded with gifts from their cruise.

For Jacob and Erika, the four days loomed over them in much the same way as the mountains loomed over Fox Run. Their grandparents' house wasn't exactly child friendly. They had no cable TV, no video games, and cell phone service was spotty on the best of days.

His temper frayed by boredom, Jacob, who'd always been overly energetic, even for a nine-year-old, made a face. "It's the same old boring story every year. Why can't we go into town and do something? Maybe see a movie?"

"Because Yule is for being with family." Grandma Anders shook a bony finger at him. "Children today have forgotten the old ways. They think only of themselves."

"*Ja.*" Grandpa Anders sucked on his empty pipe. He'd given up tobacco years before, but never the habit of clenching the pipe between his teeth while sitting by the fire. "And those are the ones who get no presents from *Jule-nissen* later tonight."

"Grandpa, we don't believe in Santa or the Easter Bunny. What makes you think we're gonna believe in an elf who rides a talking goat and leaves gifts for children?" Jacob laughed, but his grandparents didn't smile.

"Ah. No talking to children today." Grandpa Anders got up and shook his head. "Goodnight, then. If you think the tales of your ancestors are such. . . *foof*," he said, waving his hand at them, "perhaps you should stay up and watch for the *Jule-nissen* yourself."

"Maybe I will."

"Jacob, hush." Erika gave her brother a poke. Normally she wouldn't care, but with her parents gone she felt responsible for her brother, and she didn't want him being rude.

"I think perhaps bed is a good idea for all of us," Grandma Anders said, taking her teacup into the kitchen.

"No way! It's not even nine o'clock yet. We never go to bed this early at home."

"You're not at home, young man." Grandma Anders glared at him, giving him what the children secretly called her 'stink eye.' It meant she'd reached the point where she'd put up with no more nonsense. "So off to bed. Now!" She clapped her hands twice, the sudden sound like branches snapping under the weight of too much ice.

"But—"

"C'mon, Jacob. I think you had too much sugar tonight." Erika grabbed him by the arm.

"Lemme go!" He yanked himself from her grasp and stormed down the hall to the guest bedroom they were sharing.

"I'm sorry, Grandma," Erika said.

Grandma Anders patted her shoulder and planted a soft, whiskery kiss on her cheek. "Don't fret, child. Someday he will learn the truth."

*   *   *

Jacob and Erika lay awake in their room. Upstairs, the grumbling, wheezing sounds emanating from their grandparents' bedroom told them *Mormor* and *Farfar* Anders were fast asleep.

"I'm hungry," Jakob whispered.

"No, you're not. You had two plates for dinner, and at least three desserts, plus the one I saw you sneak while everyone was sitting by the fire."

"Fine. Then I'm thirsty."

Erika sighed. "What you are is bored and a brat. Go to sleep." She wished she could do the same. She'd been trying to doze off for over an hour. But too much sugar and a day of doing nothing but helping in the kitchen had her wide awake.

"Did you hear that?" Jakob asked.

"All I hear is you talking."

"Sssh!"

She started to scold him for being such a pain, and then stopped.

Because she *did* hear it.

A low, distant moaning, winter-cold and ethereal as the wind. A dozen voices; a hundred. A thousand, perhaps, all sighing at once, all lamenting a sadness older than time but not forgotten.

Jacob climbed out of bed and went to the window. His body was a gray shadow among all the others in the room. When he pulled the white lace curtain aside, he revealed a scene that was almost alien, as the snow, so white it almost glowed, hid the ordinary beneath weird mounds and featureless plains.

"Don't!" Erika couldn't explain it, but she felt something deep in her bones.

Danger waited outside.

As usual, Jacob didn't listen. He pressed his face to the glass and peered out.

"I don't see anything," he whispered.

Against her better judgment, Erika joined him at the window, barely noticing the chill of the floor against her bare feet.

Jacob's breath left twin ovals of fog on the frigid glass as he pushed closer to look up and down the street.

Shaped like a heart, Erika thought, and that scared her just as much as the distant susurrations of grief.

Outside, nothing seemed different than any other night. The houses were dark. Like the hard-working towns around it, Fox Run rose early and went to bed early.

Just when Erika thought her chattering teeth might wake her grandparents, new sounds joined the mourning dirge. A triumphant cry, accompanied by the bellow of a horn and the baying of hounds.

"Something's happening!" Before Erika could stop him, Jacob dashed from room. For a moment she stood frozen by indecision. Then she heard the slam of the back door and the spell holding her in place broke like an ice dagger snapping from the gutter.

Pausing just long enough to put on boots and grab her coat from the hook by the back door, she hurried outside and spotted Jacob already running down the road.

"Jacob, stop! Come back!" He didn't, so despite the glacial air that threatened to freeze her blood and stop her heart, Erika ran after him.

It took three blocks to catch up with Jacob, and by the time she did, her face burned and tiny icicles of snot crusted her nose and upper lip.

"I'm gonna kill you when we get back," she said, grabbing a fistful of his coat.

"Quiet!" He put a finger to his lips. "It's almost here."

Since the sounds were no louder, Erika wanted to ask him how he knew, but then she understood. He *felt* it, and she could, too.

A heartbeat later, the source of the supernatural noise appeared. Swirling towers of mist, so many she couldn't count them, appeared out of nowhere and sailed down the road as fast as racing cars. As they swept past, she glimpsed faces, twisted and horrible. The moaning of the apparitions vibrated her teeth like a dentist's drill. Next to her, Jacob pressed his hands over his ears.

The line of spirits—for she knew that's what they were—seemed to go on forever, but it was only seconds before they were past, and the reason for their wailing became apparent.

Behind them came more ghosts, mounted on ephemeral horses and surrounded by massive hounds with glowing red eyes. Leading the pack was a giant of a man wearing the antlered skull of a colossal deer as a helmet. It was his exultant war cries that had the other spirits fleeing, as he led his phantom troop in pursuit.

Ten heartbeats later, the streets lay empty again.

"Did you see that?" Jacob asked. "What were they?"

"I don't know." Erika pulled at him. "Let's go home before we freeze to death."

"'Tis not the cold you should be worrying about."

Erika screamed and Jacob gasped at the unknown voice behind them. Turning, they found themselves face to face with a goat wearing a green jacket. On its back perched a tiny man with a long, pointed beard. Like the goat, the man's yellow eyes had horizontal pupils, and he wore green clothes as well.

"*Jule-nissen*." Jacob's eyes were wide. "You're real!"

The elf shook his head. "Yes, but you'll be nothing but a memory if the Cat gets you."

"The cat? What cat?"

"The Yule Cat, sonny-boy. He's been stalking you since you left your house."

"I didn't see any—"

"There!" The elf pointed down the street.

Between two houses, a shadow, darker than the sky and impossibly huge, slid across the snow. Before Erika could think of anything to say, a giant tabby cat, taller than a lion and twice as broad, stalked into view, yellowish-green eyes glowing and a hungry smile on its face.

Jacob moaned, and the Cat, even from a hundred yards away, heard. Its ears twitched and it crouched down in the middle of the street, tail whipping back and forth behind it.

"Run," Erika said.

Jacob stood still, frozen in fear.

"Run!" This time she shouted it. At the same time, the cat sprang forward.

"This way," the elf called to them, as the goat carried him down a side street.

Jacob and Erika followed. Each step took them further from their grandparents' house, but they didn't care. All that mattered was eluding the impossible feline sprinting down the road after them.

The goat led them around a corner and Erika felt a rush of relief as the Cat skidded on the slippery road and missed the turn. Then her relief turned to horror as the Cat sprang out from behind a house and swung a massive paw that sent the goat and its elfin rider tumbling across the icy blacktop. It swung again and Jacob cried out as a white cloud exploded from his chest. Erika screamed, sure the cat had disemboweled her brother and she was watching the air from his lungs freeze as it escaped. Then she saw it was just the front of his down jacket torn open and gushing feathers into the night.

"Get up!" Erika grabbed Jacob and pulled as he kicked his legs in a frantic attempt to get his feet under himself.

The Yule cat took a half-swing at them and hot liquid ran down her legs. She remembered how Mittens, the cat they'd had when she was younger, used to play with field mice and birds the same way, toying with them until it was ready to bite their heads off.

Now she knew how they felt.

"Ho, Yule Cat! Train your eyes this way!"

Erika jumped at the *Jule-nissen's* shout. In her worry for Jacob, she'd forgotten about the elf and his goat. She watched in amazement as the diminutive man waved his arms while the goat jumped and danced on its hind legs.

"What are you doing?"

"Saving your lazy hides," the elf said. "This is your chance. Return to your house. We'll be fine."

Erika didn't argue. Hand in hand, she and Jacob ran as fast as they could, the December air burning their lungs, hearts pounding in time with their feet. They ran without looking back, deathly afraid the Cat might be only a whisker's length away.

Suddenly Jacob cut sharply to the right. Erika started to shout at him and then realized they'd reached their grandparents' house. They pounded up the front steps and flung open the door so hard it hit the wall and sent knick-knacks clattering to the floor.

"Who's there? What's going on?" Josef Anders appeared at the top of the stairs, his wife close behind him.

"Grandma! Grandpa! It's after us! The Yule Cat!"

Erika slammed the door shut and twisted the lock. Grandma Anders said something, but Erika couldn't hear over the sounds of her and Jacob gasping for air.

"Into the living room! Hurry!" Grandpa Anders hurried down the stairs and tugged at their sleeves.

"But we're safe now. The goat—" The rest of Jacob's words disappeared in a crash of breaking glass as a pumpkin-sized paw came through the window next to the door.

"There's no hiding from the Cat," Grandma Anders shouted. "Only one thing can save you. Come!"

Erika and Jacob followed their grandparents into the living room, where the sweet scent of pine still decorated the air from the Yule log smoldering in the fireplace. Behind them, the Cat let out a fierce yowl at being denied its prey yet again.

Grandma Anders grabbed two small boxes from beneath the Christmas tree. "Here, open these. Quickly now."

"What?" Erika took the box but could only stare at it. With everything that had happened, the merry green and red wrapping paper seemed unreal.

"Do as your *Mormor* says." Grandpa Anders threw an angry scowl at them as he pulled the drapes shut. With his head turned away, he never saw the movement outside the window, never knew the Yule Cat was there until it burst through the glass and knocked him sideways into a bookcase. Shaking shards from its fur, the Cat let out a roar.

"Grandpa!" Jacob cried.

Erika turned to run but her grandmother stopped her by slapping her across the face. "Open the *fordømt* box!"

Hoping the box contained some kind of magic weapon, Erika tore at the paper and cardboard. When she saw what was inside, her hands went limp and the box fell to the floor.

"A shirt?" She sank to her knees, knowing there was no hope left. Hot, fetid breath blew past her face, carrying the stench of rotten meat. Tears ran down Erika's face as she closed her eyes and waited for the end.

The carrion stink grew stronger and a whimper escaped her throat as something cold and wet bumped ever so lightly against her neck. Then it was gone.

"That's right, one for the girl and one for the boy, too. Now be gone."

Erika heard her grandmother's voice but the words didn't make sense. She opened her eyes and risked turning her head, just in time to see the Yule Cat climb out through the shattered picture window. Grandpa Anders was leaning against the bookcase, a cut on his forehead dripping blood. Jacob stood near him, his half-opened box in his hands.

Eyes still on the departing feline, Erika asked, "What happened?"

"I can answer that, young miss."

Erika turned and saw the *Jule-nissen* atop his goat, right next to Grandma Anders, who didn't seem at all surprised by their presence.

"'Twas the gifts. A shirt for each of you."

"On Yule Eve, the *Jule-nissen* leaves a gift of clothing for all the children," Jacob said in a soft voice, "except for the lazy ones."

"And for them?" the elf asked.

"The Yule Cat eats them."

"So, you did listen to my stories." Grandpa Anders put a hand on the boy's shoulder.

"You really brought us gifts?" Jacob asked.

The goat snorted and the *Jule-nissen* shook his head. "Not me. You haven't done anything to deserve them, in my eyes. But lucky for you, someone thought different, and to the Cat, a gift's a gift." The elf snapped his fingers and he and his goat disappeared in a burst of golden sparkles.

"Then who—?" Jacob looked confused, but Erika knew exactly where the gifts had come from.

"You knew the tales were true," she said to her grandmother. "You did it to protect us."

Grandma Anders gave them the briefest of smiles. "We follow tradition, even if you do not. All families make sure to keep gifts handy in case the Yule Cat appears."

"You have to be careful on Yule," Grandpa Anders said.

Jacob nodded. "'Cause of the Yule Cat."

"Yes, but not just the Cat. 'Tis also the night of the Hunt, when the spirits of the Oak King arise to drive away the spirits of the Holly King, and put an end to nights growing longer. Get in their way and you'll become like them, doomed to Hunt forever."

"The Hunt," Erika whispered. She shivered, remembering the wailings of the Holly King's spirits as the Oak King banished them until June.

Grandma Anders noticed her reaction. "Go put on dry clothes. I'll make hot cocoa."

After the children left the room, Grandma Anders went into the kitchen, where her husband was already filling a pot with milk.

"Well?" he asked.

"I think from now on they'll listen when you tell your stories."

So distant they wouldn't have heard it if not for the broken window, a child's voice screamed in pain.

Josef Anders nodded. "*Ja.* Let us hope so. For their sakes."

10
The Christmas Letter

By EmmaLee Pallai

Mama said that when the Darr mine exploded I finally fell asleep. She said I'd been up all night fussing and crying and keeping my dad and big sister, who was only two years older than me, awake. Mama said I cried straight through the night and into the day and then the Earth shook and it must have made me feel better than her rocking because I finally fell asleep. She said she didn't hear the explosion though, just felt the ground moving about. But she said she knew. She put me down in the bed and stood facing the door, knowing that something wasn't right.

I don't remember much about my daddy. Nothing really. Sometimes, when I'm out riding Jasper, my daddy's old horse, I'll smell a smell and think of what my daddy must have looked like, but don't really know if I'm thinking of him or not. My sister Beatrice, she liked to hold it over me that she remembers him cradling and reading to her. My mama, she just gets all misty-eyed when trying to talk about him. Life's not that easy with him gone. The mine-owners gave Mama some money. They buried Daddy along with all the other men up at a special place near Smithton.

Every year on December 7th, the anniversary of the explosion, I go up there with Mama and Beatrice and all the other people who lost their daddies and husbands in that mine and we say our prayers and wish their souls rest. Mama and Beatrice they cry, but not me. Sometimes I just think, *Oh well*, and look to see what the birds are doing in the trees or what bugs are crawling on the ground and I hope I can find a roly-poly to play with. I like the way they curl into little balls when I pick them up. Last time we went, I was mad. I was mad that Daddy died just before my first Christmas and that I couldn't remember him telling me stories or if he had a nice beard like Mr. Kelsen who ran the shop in town and always gave me a piece of candy when Mama wasn't looking.

Every Christmas I thought about how I never got to have him tuck me in to bed and tell me to fall sleep so that Santa Claus would come. He never read me *The Night Before Christmas* which Mama had clipped from the paper and read to us every year. I imagined his "ho, ho, ho's" must have been truer to Santa's, although she tried. I was ten-years-old and never given a present by my daddy, and sometimes that hurt. Especially when Beatrice would come downstairs each Christmas Eve with the doll that Daddy got her for her first Christmas and say how happy she was to have that as a memory of our daddy, and how it still kind of smelled like him. Not that she ever let me smell it. But, I think it was like that smell when I took Jasper out, of swamp and sweat and soot with a touch of happiness.

This past year I took to walking up to the Darr mines. Jasper got too spooked if we were near the place, so I just snuck up alone whenever I could. I hid it well, not even nosy Beatrice knew. The place is abandoned now, but I hear the spirits. Mama, she kept the articles about the explosion and I look at them from time to time, read my daddy's name out loud. One man, he got his head clean blown off and some say his body is still groping around in those caverns looking for his noggin' so he can find his final resting place. Daddy, he was farther back. He wasn't one of those found in the front of the mine, so close to freedom.

I walk around and around outside where the mine used to be and pick up rocks and wait for dusk and wonder if my daddy is still trapped in there. I wonder what his final thoughts were. Did he think of his little Frankie Jr. back home sleeping? Did he think of Mama and Beatrice?

Sometimes I'd talk to my daddy up there, usually when the sun set but just before the moon was full in the sky. That's when the spirits are strongest. I'd just sit there and talk about my day like I was really talking to my dad. "Miss Stringer at school is nice, but thinks I need to focus more on my handwriting," I'd say. "But she thinks my math shows promise. She also says I'm a real good reader. I bet I'm an even better reader than Beatrice, because she says she doesn't like to read. She's good with sewing already. I know she hates it when Mama makes her fix my clothes, but she does it real good. Mama, she's working down at the restaurant in town. She makes real good pies and biscuits for all the people who work around there. All the miners come in on Wednesdays when she makes the cakes. It's sad that she's not at home much, but sometimes I can go there after school and she'll sneak me a piece of ham and her boss, Mr. Frankel, he acts like he doesn't see it but then winks at me. He even gave me a soda once for my birthday and it was all bubbly and good."

Other times I wasn't as nice. I'd scream, "Why did you leave us, Dad? Why? We need you. Why did you leave and make Mom work? Why did you leave me with no memories and Beatrice with a few and Mama with so many she cries herself to bed some nights thinking about you? How could you do that to us, Daddy, don't you love us?" even though I knew it wasn't his fault. Sometimes I'd even yell at God for taking my daddy away. For taking so many daddies away.

After each time I talked I'd listen. I'd hear whispering in the trees and wonder if it was my daddy trying to get through from the spirit side or just the wind. I'd hear things rustling in the bushes and wonder if it was the ghost of the headless miner or just a rabbit. Sometimes I'd hear knocking, like it was coming from the other side of the mine. Those times I thought it was one of those who died trapped in there, and I'd run back home. Then sometimes I swear I'd see something, like an outline of a person. That something would look at me and mouth words and then mist away as the moon rose higher into the sky.

Christmas was coming and I couldn't stand the thought of another year with Beatrice showing off her doll that Daddy got her and me not having anything but a vague smell I thought was him. I took to spending even more time up by the Darr mines, even doing my homework up there. Now my talks were different. I was sad and the only one I could tell it to was the mine where my daddy died. "I'm sorry, Daddy," I sighed into the dirt. I was digging with a twig, writing my name over and over. Teacher said I needed to practice my writing. "I'm sorry, Daddy," I said again. "I'm sorry that when your mine exploded I slept. I'm sorry I didn't know you."

I closed my eyes and continued writing my name, the stick just moving and moving and I tried to imagine what my daddy looked like and what Christmas must have been like the day Daddy gave Beatrice her doll. I imagined what it was like to be hugged by my daddy and then I felt all warm and tingly so I opened my eyes. The sun had just set and the moon hadn't risen yet but I could see in the fading light that in the sand was written, "I love you, son." I know I didn't write that. But, there it was, above my name so it said, "I love you, son. Frank, Frank, Frank, Frank," all those times I wrote my name.

That night I went to sleep tossing and turning and wondering if it was my daddy that wrote to me. I couldn't reach that high with the stick, not where I was sitting. Plus, I didn't think it was my handwriting either. Each letter was so straight and perfect like Miss Stringer would have liked. The next morning after I did my chores I asked Mama if Daddy was good at handwriting.

"Very good," she said.

"Not like me, right?" I asked.

"Oh, you'll get better. And you're an awfully good storyteller like your daddy was. He used to write me letters whenever he got the paper." I could tell she was getting sad, but it was the good sad, the sad of remembering someone you loved.

"So he wrote all nice and straight in block letters like Miss Stringer says we need to?"

"What has you asking all this?" she said. Then she moved away to her special drawer and came back with a stack of letters. "See," she said as she unfolded one on her lap. "See how fine your daddy could write?"

Beatrice had come into the room and she sat down next to Mama and stroked her hair. She noticed Mama crying and looked at me like it was my fault, and I guess it was. But, it was also the fault of the mine for taking my daddy away. Mama read the letter to us. It was about how happy he was I was to be born and how he just knew from the kick I was a big strong boy. I almost cried hearing how much my daddy couldn't wait to meet me. Mama didn't let me touch the letter, but I got a good look at the handwriting. I also put my head close to smell it and it was the powder and soap smell of Mama mixed with the outdoors of Daddy.

I couldn't get up to the mine for a few days but on Sunday after church I snuck up. I brought a piece of biscuit with me and laid it up there for my daddy, just in case his ghost self got hungry. I told Daddy that Christmas was coming and that I'd have to listen to Beatrice again. I closed my eyes a bit and must have fallen asleep because I woke up when I felt something like a hug and written in the sand was, "Be nice to your sister." It was above where I practiced my writing so it said, "Be nice to your sister, Frank, Frank, Frank. Merry Christmas, Frank Schmidt." I knew this time it was my daddy's handwriting.

Each time I went up by the mines I felt him more. Now, there was a scent, too. That scent of outside and sweat and love that made me feel him, although I never saw him. I'd close my eyes and when I opened them there would be a message. Not every time, but most now. He told me that he missed my

Mama. When I asked him about the mine and the explosion and how bad I felt about sleeping he wrote, "Don't' feel bad. It was fast for us all. One day we was there, one day we wasn't."

Christmas was coming fast. I didn't know what to get Mama or Beatrice, or what I was going to do when Beatrice trotted out her doll and told the story of how much Daddy meant to her and how she loved that she had that little piece of him. She always looked at me when she said it, like, "See what I have and you don't?" This year I did have Daddy. I had him writing to me sometimes up by the mines. I had the smell. I had that feel of the wind—him when he hugged me. I had the words in sand that were my daddy. But I couldn't tell her. She'd just say I was jealous because she got a present from our daddy and I didn't and she'd be right, I was jealous.

"Daddy, I wish I had a nice gift from you like Beatrice," I said next time I went to the mine. It was December 23rd, Christmas Eve Eve. Then I thought about what I said. As much as I missed a daddy I never knew, Mama missed the man she married and that was worse. "I wish I had a gift for Mama," I said into the wind. I had tried to make her something pretty, even saved up and bought some special paper, but I ruined one piece already with my bad handwriting and then didn't know what to say. Every time Beatrice could she'd corner me and say how she got Mom the best present because Mrs. Jay let her have some fabric scraps and she used them to make Mom a little satchel to hold the letters from Dad safe.

On Christmas Eve proper I went up to the mines to wish Daddy a Merry Christmas. I brought him a biscuit and even a sweet potato. I didn't know if ghosts ate, but figured he might like the smell. I took up my paper and ink and pen and tried to think of a nice letter to write to Mama. Then the sun began to set and I dozed off. Suddenly, I smelled that daddy smell. I was afraid to open my eyes because what if I saw my daddy and he was like after the explosion, all burns and smoke? But, what if I kept my eyes closed and I didn't see him ever and this was my last chance? I fought to open my eyes and saw a shadow of what must have been my daddy and he was writing on the paper.

Then he folded it up and looked at me. "Give this to your mother," he said. There was another letter, too, and when he handed it to me he said, "Open this tomorrow." I asked him what I should write to Mama and he told me to just tell her I love her, that that's all people ever need on Christmas or any other day, just to be told they're loved. I was trying hard not to cry and I looked up at my daddy and asked what happens now.

"I have to go son," he said. "But I love you, and Merry Christmas."

I ran home with the paper and the ink and wanted to read the letter Daddy wrote to Mama but knew it wasn't right. I put the note he wrote me under my pillow lest I try to read it before Christmas. For Mama, I slipped it into her stocking with my letter when no one was looking.

The next morning, after breakfast, when we got to open presents, Beatrice was all sorts of smug when she presented her gift to Mama. After Mama was done cooing over the letter satchel, I brought her her stocking. She reached in and took out the letter. When she opened it, her mouth opened and then closed, like she was going to read it out loud and then thought better of it. I looked at it real quick and saw the neat crisp letters of my daddy. Tears were falling from her eyes. Then she reached into her stocking again and took out my letter, which said only, "I love you, Mama," in my not so straight letters and Mama cried even harder. She scooped me into her lap and hugged me. Beatrice started to cry for no reason and she hugged Mama, too. While Mama held me, I thought of my letter upstairs, the one Daddy wrote to me. I had read it before going down to breakfast, first thing when the sun hit my bedroom. Daddy had written that I was such a fine boy. He said to take care of Mama and Beatrice, especially at Christmas. He told me he loved me and always will.

11

Beggars at Dawn

By Elizabeth Massie

With my Mauser pistol in my canvas satchel, biscuits in my coat pocket, and my shotgun over my shoulder, I left home in the blue shadows of pre-dawn before Janet and the children had begun to stir. I thought I heard Janet mutter, "Stowe?" as I stepped out to the porch but realized it was only the squeal of the door closing and the groan of the planks beneath my cracked leather boots.

The ground was frozen, slick with the previous night's sleet. Blackened arms of naked oaks scratched the pewter sky, searching for the sun. I took the rutted road that led from our cabin toward the mining town of Blue Peak, past our empty pig barn and dead vegetable garden, on by the hut in which Mattie McAllister and her four children lived. The door to the McAllisters' hut was hung with the bit of Christmas cheer Mattie could afford—a swatch of cedar tied with one of her daughter's red hair ribbons. Mattie lived alone with her children now, her Joe having died of the black lung last February.

On down the road a ways where I veered off onto one of the vine-choked footpaths into the forest. My body was stiff with the cold; my bones ached with life. I listed heavily to my right to keep most of my weight off my bad leg.

It was mid-December, frigid in the way only the Appalachians ridges could be. There would be little to hunt. Once fall passed, deer became gaunt, ghost-like, their thin bodies blending in among the barren trees, their breaths vague on the air. I would be lucky to find one. I'd also keep my eyes open for just about anything else with meat on it. Turkeys, rabbits, squirrels, woodchucks. Creatures that hadn't been driven underground or away by the brutal winter. My family needed the meat. We wouldn't make it through Christmas and into the New Year on just a can of flour and some softening potatoes. And I was not one to shirk my duties.

I always did my duties. As a boy, a miner, a husband, a father. A soldier. Always, duties came first.

The terrain was rough, with ice-downed sycamores strewn across the path and sudden surges in the ground where heavy rains had tried to force the land into some kind of jagged moonscape. I tripped several times as pale light from the low-seated moon appeared and disappeared behind clouds. I twitched at sounds that I knew were little more creaking wood and falling water drops. Stray dead leaves, still clinging to the walnut trees, chattered like tiny teeth.

I'd come home from Europe four weeks earlier, having joined the army in May. Taking a train from the mountainside town of Grundy east to Roanoke, I'd signed up with other doughboys to fight the Germans for our country. To do my duty. I was sure nothing about war would frighten me. I'd lived through two mine collapses, bear attacks, pneumonia, and a fire that destroyed my parents' cabin, taking my grandfather with it.

How much we think we know. How much we really don't.

My time over there was cut short. I shot a few Germans from a distance and killed two up close, one with my blade and a second with my hands down in the mud of St Mihiel, France. The German had stared up at me, his lips curled and his pupils tiny with the thrill of the fight. I wrenched the Mauser off him when I was done and then stood, shaking uncontrollably, to rejoin my fellows. In that moment a bullet slammed into my shoulder, a second into my thigh. I dropped, hard.

They hustled me back stateside to Camp Devens outside Boston, where

I discovered men who weren't dying from war injuries but from the Spanish flu.

Where was my duty then? The army had no more need of me. I didn't want to lie there and die the way many of those poor boys did, strangling from muck in their lungs and begging for mercy with their eyes. I left with my discharge against the advice of doctors, who were no longer my superiors, and bummed a ride on a southbound train. I hitched a ride from Grundy up to Harman Junction, and then hiked the rest of the way home. It took a long time. My leg oozed blood much of the way.

Janet was shocked to see me trudging toward our cabin, my face streaked with soot, bleeding, limping. She raced to me, squeezed me until I thought I couldn't breathe, sobbing that she'd heard reports of the flu and how many had died. Knowing I was in Camp Devens, she had prayed every night that I would be spared.

She bound my wound and fed me well that evening. The last of the ham from the summer hog. Biscuits. Fried apples and squash. The children—eight-year-old Stead, six-year-old Sally, and five-year-old Sid—watched in awe as I ate, their gazes flickering between my mouth and the deep pit in my shoulder. I told them a German had taken a bite out of me, but I'd taken an even bigger bite out of him. Stead and Sally giggled; Sid continued to stare.

I was among my own again, not in a soggy, foul trench with New Yorkers or Californians or Texans. I was ready to return to the mine even with my stiffened arm and ravaged leg, ready to do my duty as a miner.

A mottled turkey fluttered across the path ahead of me, startled from its roost. I aimed my shotgun, fired, missed. Cedar bark sprayed the air. I cursed, loaded, and aimed again but the bird was long gone.

Overhead a crow called, "Uh-oh, uh-oh."

Up an incline then down the other side, losing my balance and grabbing thorny saplings to stay upright. My chapped hands were gouged, the sleeves of my jacket ripped.

Red Allen, the Blue Peak Mine foreman, told me two days after my return that he had no more need of me now that I was crippled. I said I would get better. He said he was sorry but didn't have time to wait me out. It'd been my decision to take off to war, as patriotic as that was. He'd already filled my job with another man from the other side of the mountain, who had moved to town not long ago. One who had two good legs under him. Red patted my back and shook my hand. His palm was clammy.

No more paycheck. No pension. No more provisions from the company store. An offer from the church ladies to bring suppers on Fridays.

I forced myself up yet another incline where I stopped, folded over at the waist, and hissed in a sudden torrent of pain and despair. Air rushed in through my open mouth. It tasted like iron and impending snow.

"Uh-oh," called the crows.

After a moment, I slowly raised my head to squint left and right through the fluttering darkness. I realized I was atop the old Virginia and Tennessee rail bed. A quarter-mile west of here was the train tunnel that was built in 1859. The train track was torn up and the tunnel abandoned after a cave-in convinced the rail barons to move this section of track a mile to the south and build a new tunnel.

I'd discovered the old tunnel as a boy, though the warnings of my aunts and grandfather put a fear in me that kept me at a safe distance from its stone and brick walls.

The tunnel's haunted, Stowe, they said.

Haunted with what? I wanted to know.

Just don't go, was always the answer.

I started down the rail bed, along the relatively flat stretch into the canopy of trees that hung low with frost. I wanted to go down there, to the tunnel. For some reason, I needed to go there. It made no sense, but I knew I had to do just that.

Digging a biscuit from my pocket, I took a bite. It was hard as a stone, which was odd because Janet always cooked the lightest soda biscuits around Blue Peak. She'd learned how from her Mama. This one hurt my jaw and scraped the insides of my cheeks.

Janet, what happened to the biscuits? How old are they?

Forcing down the biscuit bits, I adjusted the satchel and shotgun on my shoulders, and headed off toward the tunnel.

It appeared like a dragon's lair in a dream, not there and suddenly there, around a slight curve and flanked by two steep, granite slopes. It was as I remembered it to be though seeming even a bit larger. A stone-lined arch twenty-five feet wide and thirty feet tall, sewn in place with a tapestry of browned Virginia creeper and poison ivy. Long, pointed icicles hung from the apex like glistening fangs. The tunnel emitted a cold mist that obscured anything that might be inside.

Slowly, I limped to the tunnel's misty maw. Fungus-scented air licked my face. The icicles high above dripped down into my hair, tickling it like spider legs. I slapped the water away and stepped inside.

My hand instinctively reached around to the satchel with the Mauser pistol. I could feel its outline through the canvas, remembering the way it looked in the German's hand and then in mine. The way it sounded when I fired it. Loud. Certain.

I didn't know why I'd brought it with me. I would never use it for hunting. I unbuckled the satchel, drew out the Mauser, cocked it, and engaged the safety.

I moved into the mist of the tunnel, listening.

For what? There were no animals here, save a few bats, snakes, and millipedes. Nothing worthy of a Christmas dinner, even for the poorest of the poor.

In several more yards now, holding the pistol before me. I should leave. I should go out and find food. There was no reason to be here.

Except that I wanted to be. The dank air felt right. In spite of its chill and its smells of decay, it seemed as though the place welcomed me, expected me. I closed my eyes for a moment, taking it in. I knew this feeling, these smells. They were intimately familiar. But from where? From when?

Then I remembered.

The trenches at St Mihiel. September 13th, 1918. The stench of a foreign rain, tank engines overheating as they negotiated the knee-deep mud, blood leeching into the earth, infected feet, mildewed uniforms.

Jesse, my buddy, dead in front of me. Andrew, my buddy, dead behind me. Me, bleeding from my arm and my leg. But not dead. I should have been dead. Like them, I should not have come home. It would have been my duty to stay away. To never come back.

But why? I drove the heel of my free hand into my forehead, hard. *Why should I have died there?*

Something cracked to my right and I whipped about, my leg flaring hot with the motion. The mist had filled in the space where I had been, thickening to where I could no longer see the entrance, only a faint gray glow beyond. Day was trying to break.

My heart thundered. I stood, waiting.

"Who is there?" My own voice startled me. My scalp tightened.

"Hello, Stowe."

I gasped.

"I know why you're here." The voice was in the mist, deep in the thick purple-gray tapestry, a whisper so soft I could hardly hear it. Young. Very young.

"Stead? Is that you?"

Silence.

"Stead, son, are you here?"

Silence.

It was my imagination. Stead couldn't be here. It was impossible. I squeezed my eyes shut. But why? Why couldn't he have followed me here?

Because he was asleep. He, Janet, and the others were still sleeping.

Aren't they?

I gripped the pistol tightly.

"Stowe." The voice was a little louder now. A bit older than Stead.

"Who is that?"

Something moved in the mist, just beyond me.

"Tell me who you are or I'll kill you!" I demanded.

I saw his face then, appearing through the gray, an angular face, with a reddish beard and large dark eyes. He looked to be about seventeen. His brow was furrowed in that almost delicate way of worried young men who are years away from wrinkles.

"They need you," he said. "Go home, Stowe."

I licked mist and salt from my lips. I didn't know him. He could be an insane man, hiding here in the tunnel. I knew about crazy people. My grandfather was crazy as a bedbug. He used to sit on the porch of our cabin and scream that the Yankees were watching him from the trees, aiming at him, determined to bring him down since he had survived the War Between the States.

"Get away," I said.

"Don't do it. They need you."

"Don't do what? What are you talking about?"

He nodded toward my right hand, and I felt it then. The muzzle of the pistol was against my temple. I had put it there without knowing.

"Don't do it, Stowe, please."

But oh, did it feel right. Pressed there, cool, kind, ready to kiss my torment away. Take it all away. To do my final duty. To pay for what I'd done.

But what did I do...?

The man stepped closer. The mist parted and I could see his clothing. It was fashioned as if he were living a good fifty years ago. Loose linen trousers with a checked pattern. A long, brown frock coat. When he shifted he flickered, as though I was watching him through a slightly warped pane of glass.

"My family needed me but I was a coward," he said. "I was afraid to stay at home. We'd heard tell of the vicious battle over in Charleston on September 13th and I was sure the Yankees were going to come our way next, across our mountain and burn us all down, take me away to join with them or shoot me if I refused. I can't fight, Stowe. I just can't do it. Not everybody can be a soldier."

"No," I said.

"My mama and daddy, they were both ailing, ailing bad. But I told them I couldn't stay. I had to get away and hide."

My index caressed the trigger on the pistol and then I flicked off the safety with my thumb. The young man looked at it and then at me.

"I was a pathetic, yellow dog."

"You were scared."

"I hid here. I didn't care what happened outside the tunnel as long as I was safe. But the second morning there was a rumble and the tunnel came down on top of me. My parents never knew what happened to me." He paused, and held up his hand, waved it back and forth. It trailed an odd light, like that of a falling star. "So you see, not only did I harm myself, but left my parents to die alone. Not from Yankee torches or sabers, they never came close, but from illness. From loneliness."

I blinked. My heart caught. "Do you mean you're...?"

He nodded. "Yes. But you don't need to be. Don't do what you came here to do, Stowe. They need you back there. Back at Blue Peak."

Anger flared up in me from deep inside, hot and huge. "What do you mean, what I came to do?"   I cried.

"That." The young man nodded again at my pistol. "You want it to be gone, you want to forget..."

"I haven't forgotten anything! I remember it all, the mud and the screams and the bullets and the tanks!"

"Your mind remembers some," he said simply, "but your soul remembers it all."

"What...?" But then my soul opened and it all came back to me, slamming into my mind, crashing down upon me, driving me to my knees in the wet and the stink.

"I brought it with me! Oh, my God! I brought it home with me!"

I'd returned home in early November. My family had welcomed me with cheers and kisses. Within two days of my homecoming, Janet and Sid were sick. Sally and Stead followed the next morning. Four days later, they all were dead of the flu. I had brought it home to them.

I buried them behind the house.

They were gone. The biscuits in my pocket, from the last batch Janet made while she was still alive. Four weeks ago.

"I killed my family!" I screamed to the mist above me. Bile burned my throat and tears cut the corners of my eyes. "Janet, Stead, Sally, Sid. Forgive me for what I did!"

"No" said the young man. "You didn't kill them. The disease did."

I squeezed the pistol grip and shoved the muzzle so hard against my skull that I saw stars. "I have to do my duty! I have to join them!"

"You have a new duty," said the young man. "Mattie and her children.

Your neighbors."

I stared at him, my body shuddering.

"Mattie won't make it another winter without help, Stowe. You can help her. She is your family, too, and her children. We are all one family, don't you know that? Regardless of time, regardless of birth. Regardless of state or nation. Brothers. Sisters. All of us. Your duty's changed. It's not to take yourself out of the world but to stay and help them."

"I can't! The disease will get them! I holed myself up to keep away from other people! I chased Mattie off my porch several times. I didn't want her harmed! I only came out of the cabin because we needed some meat. I…I needed some meat…"

The young man shook his head, light trailing with the movement. He smiled for the first time, and it was startlingly beautiful. "The disease is gone now. It's safe. You're safe."

I knelt there, panting, sobbing. Then, when the crying had eased to a faint hitching, I forced myself to my feet. With sweat-slick hands, I re-engaged the safety, gently let the hammer down, and placed the pistol into the satchel. "All right. I'll do it." I would go to Mattie and help care for her and her children. It was my duty. As a man.

"Good."

I began to turn away, but then looked back. He still stood there in the mist. "But how did you know about me?" I asked. "How could you?"

The young man shrugged. "As I am now, I know everything that goes on around our mountains. I can't leave here, but see things in my mind and in my soul."

"But why can't you leave, too?"

He blinked, glanced away, and then looked at me again. "Because of what I did. I was wrong. I must stay here until…" his voice faded.

"Until what?"

He just considered me with his large, dark eyes. And then I knew.

"Your story needed to be told," I said. "Someone had to hear it. Some-one needs to tell it beyond this tunnel, so they'll know."

"Yes."

"But no one would ever come in here because they believed it to be haunted."

He nodded. There were tears in his eyes now, bright as crystals.

"What's your name?"

"Gregory," he said.

"I'll tell your story, Gregory. I'll let them know what happened to you."

"Thank you."

"And though your parents can't do it, I forgive you, Gregory. As your brother, I can at least do that for you. For what you did for me."

Gregory lowering his head. "May God bless you and send you a happy New Year."

Then he was gone. Vanished. Mist to mist. Spirit to spirit.

"And God send you a happy New Year," I whispered.

I went out into the world. Fat, white flakes drifted down from the early morning sky, coating the tree branches, the dead grasses, the stretch of rail bed ahead of me. Crows pecked at the earth, then turned their anxious faces toward me to beg for crumbs. I threw the biscuits from my coat pocket. They would soften in the snow.

All would soften with the new day. All would heal.

I broke a branch of holly from the craggy stone beside the rail bed. It would look nice on Mattie's front door.

Other Great Titles From

WOODLAND PRESS

Woodland Press, LLC

w w w . w o o d l a n d p r e s s . c o m

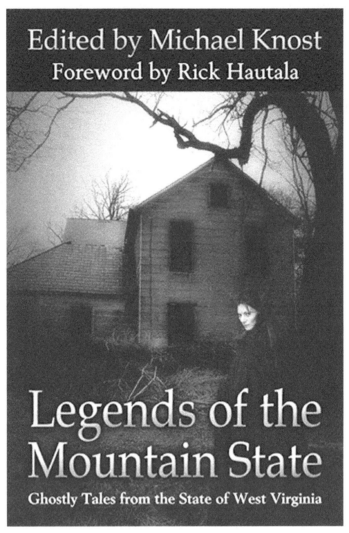

Edited by Michael Knost
Foreword by Rick Hautala

Legends of the Mountain State

Ghostly Tales from the State of West Virginia

This anthology includes thirteen accounts of ghostly manifestations, myths, and mountain mythology, based on known legends from the eerie state of West Virginia. Horror writer Michael Knost serves as the anthology's editor. Participating writers are an amalgamation of professional authors and professionals in the horror, science fiction, and fantasy fields, along with up-and-coming writers from Appalachia. Many contributors are National Bram Stoker Award winning authors currently in the national spotlight. This title is suitable for anyone who enjoys bone-chilling ghost tales told by some of the best storytellers in the business. Softcover. $18.95

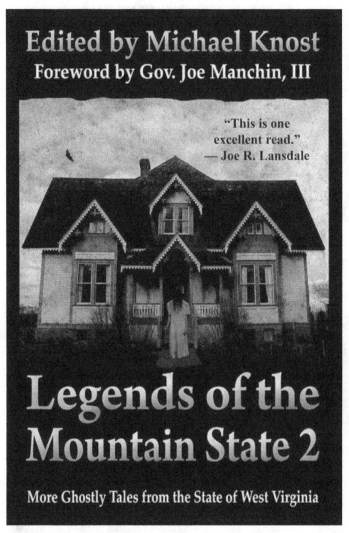

Edited by Michael Knost

Foreword by Gov. Joe Manchin, III

"This is one excellent read."
— Joe R. Lansdale

Legends of the Mountain State 2

More Ghostly Tales from the State of West Virginia

After putting together this anthology's predecessor, above, editor Michael Knost realized he had barely scratched the surface with Appalachian folklore. After seeing great success with the initial project, Woodland Press asked Knost to put together a second edition—one that focused on 13 additional ghost stories and mountain legends. The new project, which is arguably even scarier than its predecessor, embodies the same tone and texture of its forerunner, with nationally known authors and storytellers getting involved. According to Knost, this new volume offers fresh meat to those who devoured the stories in the first volume. Softcover. $14.95

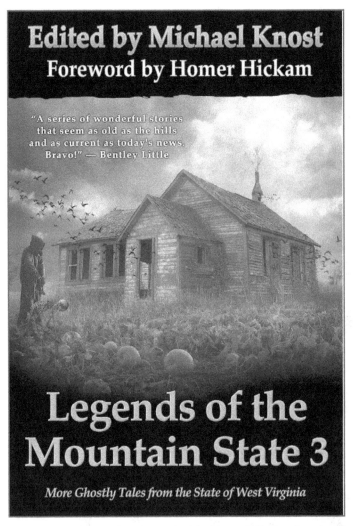

Edited by Michael Knost

Foreword by Homer Hickam

"A series of wonderful stories that seem as old as the hills and as current as today's news. Bravo!" — Bentley Little

Legends of the Mountain State 3

More Ghostly Tales from the State of West Virginia

The third installment of the *Legends of the Mountain State* series, above, is already being called the most amazing of the ghostly trilogy. Michael Knost again takes the reins as chief editor and coordinator. Here you'll find 13 final chapters—bone-chilling ghost tales and treacherous legends. Stories are penned by many of the preeminent writers in the business—National Bram Stoker Award winners, nationally known horror writers, and gifted Appalachian storytellers. The tone in this project is perhaps darker, tales creepier, and the overall texture even grittier than the first two installments. Foreword by Homer Hickam. Order *Legends of the Mountain State 3* today. Softcover. $18.95

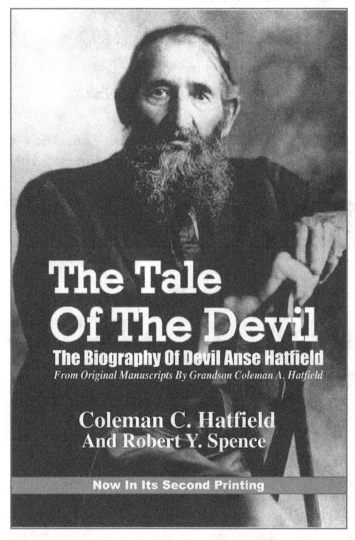

The Tale of the Devil represents the first biography of feudist Anderson "Devil Anse" Hatfield, written by great-grandson Dr. Coleman C. Hatfield (2004 Tamarack Author of the Year), and Mountain State historian Robert Y. Spence. Now in its third printing, this book remains an Appalachian best-seller. This biography of Devil Anse Hatfield faithfully documents his Civil War service as a Confederate soldier and leader of the fighting Wildcats militia, and tells the true story of the Hatfield-McCoy feud, the violent killings, and the post-feud years after the fighting ceased. Handsome Hardbound. $29.95

Writers Workshop of Horror

"A veritable treasure trove of information for aspiring writers, straight from the mouths of today's top horror scribes!"

— *Rue Morgue Magazine*

"Packing more knowledge and sound advice than four years' worth of college courses... It's focused on the root of your evil, the writing itself."

— Fangoria Magazine

"Entertaining, informative, and also plain old fun, this book will not only make you want to write more, it will give you the tools to write better. This should be mandatory reading in creative writing classes."

— Horror World

Writers Workshop of Horror focuses solely on honing the craft of writing. It includes solid advice, from professionals of every publishing level, on how to improve one's writing skills. The volume edited by Michael Knost includes contributions by a dream-team of nationally known authors and storytellers, many Bram Stoker Award winners. Contributors to this work include: Clive Barker, Joe R. Lansdale, F. Paul Wilson, Ramsey Campbell, Thomas F. Monteleone, Deborah LeBlanc, Gary A. Braunbeck, Brian Keene, Elizabeth Massie, Tom Piccirilli, Jonathan Maberry, Tim Waggoner, Mort Castle, G. Cameron Fuller, Rick Hautala, Scott Nicholson, Michael A. Arnzen, J.F. Gonzalez, Michael Laimo, Lucy A. Snyder, Jeff Strand, Lisa Morton, Jack Haringa, Gary Frank, Jason Sizemore, Robert N. Lee, Tim Deal, Brian Yount, and others. Softcover $21.95

Appalachian Case Study: UFO Sightings, Alien Encounters and Unexplained Encounters. The state of West Virginia has a long prominent history of unexplained happenings and bizarre sightings of unidentified flying objects (UFOs). This fascinating literary work researches and documents sixteen unusual UFO sightings in Appalachia. The book also includes fascinating interviews with certain West Virginia citizens who have experienced the unexplainable. Author Kyle Lovern includes an exclusive interview with nationally-known and respected UFOlogist and nuclear physicist Stanton Friedman. This title has received a great deal of national attention as the focus on UFO data shifts toward Appalachia. Softcover. $12.95

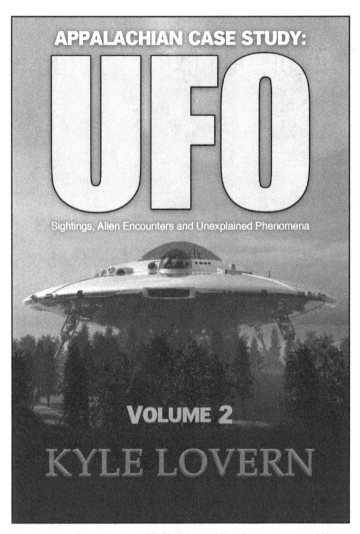

Appalachian Case Study: UFO Sightings, Alien Encounters and Unexplained Encounters - Volume 2. In this new release from Woodland Press. which is a sequel to a bestselling title about strange UFO sightings and bizarre alien abductions, UFOlogist Kyle Lovern focuses and broadens his scope as he researches and fully documents a variety of new UFO encounters, and revisits some famous sightings of yesteryear, that have taken place in Appalachia—in West Virginia, Virginia, Kentucky and Ohio. Softcover. $15.95

Be sure both volumes of *Appalachian Case Study: UFO Sightings, Alien Encounters and Unexplained Phenomena are* in your home library.

WEST VIRGINIA
TOUGH BOYS

REVISED EDITION

VOTE BUYING, FIST FIGHTING
AND A PRESIDENT NAMED JFK

F. KEITH DAVIS

Foreword by WV Senate President - Lieutenant Governor Earl Ray Tomblin

West Virginia Tough Boys. A regional bestseller, *West Virginia Tough Boys* remains a historically significant literary effort about mountain politics and the 1960 presidential primary campaign in the state of West Virginia. Rich and straightforward stories of political tomfoolery, vote-buying and eventual victory for Senator John F. Kennedy in the Mountain State's primary are documented here, as well as the making of a Mountain politician. West Virginia has often been sited as the most important and vital win in Kennedy's original bid for the White House. The book features indepth interviews and discussions with a variety of politicians and campaign workers from yesteryear. Softcover. $19.95

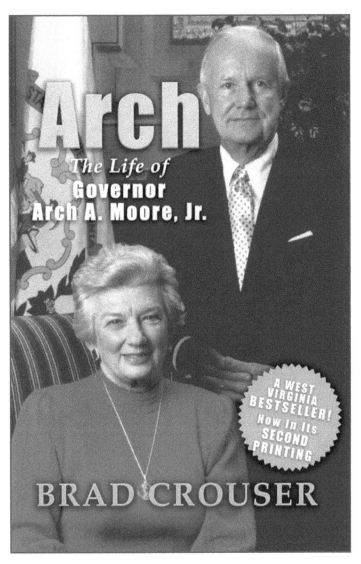

ARCH: The Life of Governor Arch A. Moore, Jr. This book is the authorized story of West Virginia Governor Arch A. Moore, Jr. Author Brad Crouser, a Charleston lawyer and former state tax commissioner, takes the reader on a fascinating journey, from the turn of the Twentieth Century and Arch's grandfather, the entrepreneur F. T. Moore, to the present day of his Congresswoman daughter, Shelley Moore Capito, from the mountaintops of triumph to the valleys of tragedy. Now in its second printing, this volume should be in every personal library. 612 Page Softcover. $32.95

The Secret Life and Brutal Death of Mamie Thurman. It was over seventy-eight years ago that this nasty homicide grabbed national headlines. This book takes a close look at this puzzling account. A regional bestseller, this book has been dubbed the "Hillbilly Dalia." It's a gruesome thriller and true account about a prominent, Depression era woman—a carry-over from the flapper age—found brutally and sadistically murdered in the heart of the Bible-belt. It was the last year of Prohibition. Mamie Thurman was a member of the tight-lipped, local aristocracy that frequented a private club in downtown Logan, WV—a wild speakeasy. She lived a risky lifestyle. Now new evidence points to several groups—from the mob to the KKK, from rumrunners to a slew of local merchants—as having a part in this true-crime. Softcover. $15.95

The Feuding Hatfields & McCoys. This unique book is about two proud families. *The Feuding Hatfields & McCoys* is a title that includes a comprehensive timeline of the feuding Hatfield family migration westward and documents the history before, during, and following the bloody feud era. Included are stories—which have never before been published—that have been collected from the Hatfield family over the years. These chapters add color and clarity to this famous vendetta. Author Dr. Coleman C. Hatfield was the great-grandson of Anderson "Devil Anse" Hatfield and was a noted Mountain State historian. Softcover. $18.95

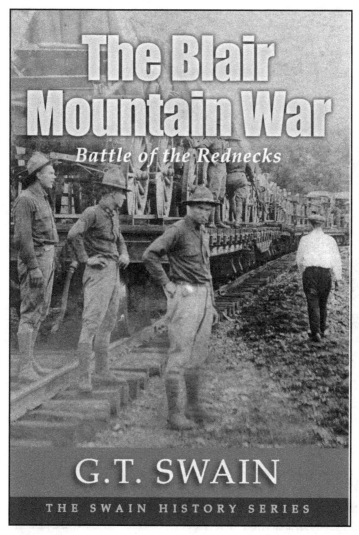

The Blair Mountain War: Battle of the Rednecks, tells the true story of the Blair Mountain War, the largest organized armed uprising in US labor history. At the time of this original manuscript, written in 1927, G.T. Swain was a reporter for The Logan County Banner, in Logan, WV. Here Swain paints a vivid picture, in his most unique style, and documents the accounts surrounding the 1921 Blair Mountain War. The WV State Archives has since stated that the mine wars have demonstrated the inability of the state and federal governments to defuse the situations short of initiating armed intervention. This is certainly true. Regardless, the details behind The Blair Mountain War remain fascinating and controversial. $12.50

Princess Aracoma and the Settling of West Virginia. Upon the tragic death of Chief Cornstalk in 1774, the Shawnees followed Cornstalk's daughter, Princess Aracoma, into present-day Midelburg Island in Logan County, West Virginia. This book aptly describes the settling of the Mountain State and explains how Princess Aracoma resolved a difficult conflict between the American Indian population and the region's earliest settlers. This title was originally authored by journalist and historian G.T. Swain in 1927. The end result is a true story and an exciting adventure, involving Indian Princess Aracoma, that takes place upon the immense backdrop of American history. $12.95

VISIT
www.woodlandpress.com
for more information on your favorite
Woodland Press authors and book titles

118 Woodland Drive, Suite 1101
Chapmanville, WV 25508

Email: woodlandpressllc@mac.com

CPSIA information can be obtained
at www.ICGtesting.com
Printed in the USA
LVHW051730261020
669856LV00004B/866